Happy New Year
2

Happy New Year 2

BY

TRACY WILSON

Published by
Beautiful Publications LLC
Stratford, CT 06614

Library of Congress Control Number:
2023900354
Print ISBN: 979-8-9871005-5-4
Ebook ISBN: 979-8-9871005-4-7

Printed in the United States of America

"Good morning..." I greeted as I came in...

"Hey – I thought you were going to be working 9 to 5?" Veronica asked...

"I am – but I always get in a little early so I can enjoy my breakfast and my coffee..." I answered as I took off my coat...

"Good morning..." Ron greeted as he came in...

"Good morning..." Veronica and I both said. Ron swiped in and went back out the door...

"Did you see that?" I nodded and didn't say anything. I opened my breakfast, took out my coffee, and opened my email...

"Did you get the emails I sent you?"

"I'll look at that at 9..." Veronica understood and went back to work...

"I'm back..." Ron said as he came back inside. I looked at the time and made a note that he returned at 8:50...

"Good morning..." Steph greeted as he came in...

"Good morning..." Veronica and I both said. Ron had a mouth full of food so he just waved. I opened Microsoft word and drafted a memo...

To: Ronald Nelson
From: Chelle Robinson
Date: Friday, January 6th, 2023
Subject: Failure To Follow Directive

Per our discussion on Wednesday, January 4th, we discussed changes that I would be making as your new supervisor. One of the changes I advised would be going into effect immediately was that there would be no clocking in and then immediately going out for coffee.

This morning you ignored that directive when you clocked in at 8:35, went out for coffee, and didn't return to work until 8:50.

Not only will you be charged 15 minutes personal leave, but a copy of this memo will also be placed in your personnel file. Hopefully this is something we won't need to address in the future.

Cc: Stephen Richardson
       County Personnel

I got up to print out the memo, printed it, picked it up, and went into Steph's office...

"Yes Chelle?"

"I need to run something by you..." I said as I showed him the memo. Steph read the memo and laughed...

"I knew it..."

"You knew he was going to do this?"

"Yes..."

"Is it okay if I write him up?"

"Absolutely..."

"Thank you..." I said as I took the memo and went back to my desk. I signed the memo, logged into leave management, took 15 minutes personal leave from his time, and added the following note: Per memo dated 1/5/23. I hit submit and got up to make copies of the memo...

"Excuse me – why did you take 15 minutes of my personal time?"

"It's explained in this memo..." I answered as I handed him the memo...

"Failure to follow directive?! Are you serious?!"

"Yes I am..." I answered as I went to give Steph a copy of the memo... "I'll be right back – I'm taking this over to personnel..."

"We have T/A mail right outside..."

"I know..." I acknowledged as I put the copy of the memo in an interoffice envelope. Steph nodded his head in acknowledgement as I left the office...

"I can't believe that Bitch wrote me up!" Ron exclaimed...

"If you don't want to be written up again I suggest you change your tone..." Steph warned. Ron and Veronica looked at him in shock...

"Veronica – please make sure you finish what Chelle asked – I need reception to be notified right away..."

"I already finished it..."

"Did you cc Ron?"

"Yes..."

"Cc me on what?!" Ron snapped...

"Check your email..." she answered as Steph went back into his office...

"Good morning Chelle..." Victoria greeted as I walked in...

"Good morning – I need to drop off this memo..." I said...

"You know you have T/A mail over at 85 – right?"

"I also know that everything that gets put in T/A mail doesn't stay in T/A mail..."

"Are you telling me you've seen people take things out of T/A mail?"

"Not since I've become a supervisor..." I answered as I put the interoffice envelope in her box..."

"Care to elaborate?"

"I need to get back to work – have a nice day Victoria..." I said as I hurried out of her office...

When I got back, Veronica was the first to greet me...

"Chelle – I sent that memo..."

"Did you cc Ron?"

"I sure did!" she exclaimed as she smiled...

"Thanks - I need you to go over the stats and the last monthly report with me when you get a chance..."

"Can we do that when I get back from lunch?"

"Sure – what time are you going to lunch?"

"I'm leaving now..."

"Okay – I'll see you later..."

"Steph – Veronica just left to go to lunch – I need her to go over the stats and monthly report with me – can I go to lunch at 2?"

"I'd rather you go at 1 – I don't want to get in the habit of letting you go to lunch after 2 – especially because you wrote Ron up..."

"You're right..."

"Speaking of that – Why didn't you put that memo in T/A mail?"

"I wanted to make sure it got to personnel..."

"I'm sure it would've gotten there..."

"I've seen people take things out of T/A mail addressed to personnel..."

"Wow..."

"Please don't ask me to tell on anybody..."

"I won't – but now that you mentioned it – I wouldn't put it past Ron..."

"I wouldn't either - "When are you going to lunch?"

"I'm going at 1..."

"Okay – I'll let you get back to what you were doing..." I said as I went back to my desk and began to organize my files. Ron stormed out the office promptly at 11:58...

"Girl!" Veronica exclaimed as she came inside. I shook my head no and Veronica understood...

"I'm going to lunch – I'll see you when I get back..." I said as I got up and left behind Steph...

"Now I gotta go cover reception again since she took you out the rotation..." Ron sighed as he came back from lunch. Veronica didn't respond... "Veronica – could you please do me a favor?"

"No she can't..." I answered as I came back in...

"I thought you were at lunch?" Veronica asked...

"I am – I forgot something..." I said as I went to my desk...

"Anyway – Veronica – could you please do me a favor and help me finish scanning?"

"No Veronica cannot help you finish scanning..." I answered...

"I wasn't talking to you!"

"When we discussed the changes I'd be making – I specifically said – effective immediately – Veronica wouldn't be helping you with your work – you've already been written up one for failure to follow a directive – would you like to be written up again?"

"This some bullshit!" he exclaimed...

"That's the last time you're going to take that tone or use that language when you speak to me or anyone else in this office!" I exclaimed...

"I'll talk anyway I feel like it and you can't do shit!"

"You keep it up and I'll initiate a section 75..."

"A section 75?! What's that?!"

"That's where you can be brought up on charges for not doing your job..."

"I do my job!"

"If you did your job – as you say – you wouldn't be asking Veronica to help you finish your work – if you think I'm playing – try me!" Veronica put her hand over her mouth as her eyes widened. Ron sat at his desk, snatched the pile, and began scanning... "I'm going back out – I might be a little late getting back from lunch – please let Steph know Veronica..." I said as I got my bag and went back out...

"Chelle – I need to see you..." Steph said when I came back inside. As soon as I got in his office I started apologizing...

"I'm sorry Steph – I forgot something and..."

"Stop..."

"Okay..."

"Veronica told me what happened..."

"Oh..."

"You know a section 75 isn't as simple as it sounds..."

"I know that – but Ron doesn't know that..."

"I just wanted you to be aware..."

"He's testing me..."

"I know he is..."

"First he went out for coffee after I specifically said get your coffee before you come to work..."

"You told him to get his coffee before he comes to work?"

"Yes – and when he said it'll make him late for work I told him to leave earlier..."

"He didn't expect you to be here early..."

"Exactly – and I also told him in front of Veronica – effective immediately Veronica isn't going to be helping him finish his work..."

"Yea – he doesn't like you..." Steph laughed...

"He had the nerve to ask me why Veronica can't help him do his work and I asked him if he helped Veronica with her work..."

"Oh wow –he knows exactly what he's doing..."

"Did Veronica tell you how he spoke to me?"

"No..."

"First he said this some bullshit – I told him that's the last time he was going to take that tone and speak to me or anyone else like that..."

"He's getting out of hand..."

"So then he tells me he'll talk anyway he feels like and I won't do shit..."

"He said that?!"

"Yes..."

"That's it – I'm writing him up!"

"Don't write him up..."

"Why not?!"

"Because I told him if he thinks I'm playing – try me!"

"Okay fine – but he only has one more time and that's it – doesn't matter what you say..."

"I'm going to go sit with Veronica and go over the stats and monthly reports..." I said as I got up and left his office. As soon as I got back to my desk, I received a notification in my phone...

"Hey Chelle,

I need you to put in for PL on Monday – I have a surprise for you.

I'll meet you at Starbucks on the corner of Court & Main at 10 a.m.

I love you.

Darnell"

I smiled as I put the phone down on my desk...
"You still wanna go over the stats?" Veronica asked...
"Yea – I just need to take care of something right quick..." I answered as I went into leave management, put in a request for PL for Monday. I waited for Steph to approve the request and once he did, I logged out... "Okay – let's get started..." I sighed as I opened up the stats...

"Where are we going?" I asked...

"You'll see..." he answered as he took my hand and we began walking down Main Street towards the Galleria. When we got closer to the train station, I knew something was up...

"We're getting on the train..." I sighed. Darnell looked over at me and smiled. He knew what his smile did to me and he enjoyed every second of it...

"Soon..." he whispered in my ear and it went straight down my spine...

"C'mon!" I exclaimed as I pulled him towards the train station...

"The next train to Grand Central Terminal will be coming next on Track 2..." I watched Darnell purchase the tickets on the app on his phone as the train pulled up on the platform. We got on the train and sat down. I snuggled up under Darnell and put my head on his chest as he wrapped his arm around my back...

"Ticket's please..." the conductor commanded...

"Good afternoon..." Darnell greeted...

"Good afternoon – tickets please..." Darnell took his phone out, activated the tickets, and showed the conductor his phone..."

"Thank you – you're all set..." the conductor stated as he walked up to the next set of passengers... "Tickets please..."

"Well hello to you too!" the man snapped...

"Hello – tickets please..." Darnell laughed and shook his head as the conductor went on his way...

"Grand Central next and final stop..." I sat up and Darnell could tell I was excited. We got off the train and Darnell took my hand as he led me through the station and outside on Madison Avenue. We continued walking until we got to Madison and East 43rd Street. I stood there waiting with him until Bus M3 pulled up...

"Are we getting on the M3?"

"Yes..."

"Okay..." We got on the bus, sat down, and I looked out the window...

"We're getting off next stop..."

13

"Okay..."   When we got to Madison and East 55th Street, we got off the bus and Darnell took my hand again. I loved that Darnell enjoyed walking as much as I did and I was happy to be in New York City...

"We're here..." he said as we stopped in front of the St. Regis Hotel. I couldn't believe I was at one of the most beautiful hotels in the city. We walked into the lobby and I was in awe... "C'mon..." he said as he led me towards the elevator...

"We don't have to check in?"

"No..." he answered as the elevator doors opened. We went inside and as soon as the doors closed, we were all over each other...

"Mmmph...   Mmmph...   Mmmph..."   I couldn't wait to get in our room so he could take me...

"This is my floor..." he said as the doors opened...

"Your floor?"

"C'mon – I'll explain after we go inside..." he answered as he led me down the hall to Unit 1021...

"Oh   my   God –   this   is   beautiful!"   I exclaimed...

"I own a share in this condo..."

"You own a share? Like a time-share?"

"It's actually better than a time-share..."

"How?"

"I actually have a deed to a fractional share of this property..."

"I still don't get it..."

"Come sit down..." he said as he led me over to the sofa. I sat down and he went into the kitchen. He came back with two tall glasses of ginger ale, set them on the coasters on the table, and sat down beside me... "Let's say it's your birthday..."

"Happy Birthday to me..." I laughed as I took a sip of ginger ale..."

"Happy Birthday..." he said as he took a sip of ginger ale and set the glass down...

"Okay – it's my birthday..."

"It's your birthday. You want to go to a restaurant you've always wanted to go to. Your friends decide to surprise you and they take you out to this restaurant for your birthday..."

"Okay..."

"You eat, drink, appetizers, entrees, and dessert. Now the check comes and it's $1,000..."

"Ooohhh..."

'Your friends chip in and each one pays about $150 a piece..."

"Oh that's nice..."

"Exactly..."

"So... You pay part of the HOA fees and taxes – but not all of it?"

"Exactly..."

"So... You all own this condo?"

"You got it..."

"So... Do I have to worry about anyone walking in on us?" Darnell smiled at me mischievously and I got excited...

"Realtor.com explains how it works in the listing. My share gives me 28 days and includes fixed week 36..."

"I'm confused..."

"Week 36 is during the U.S. Open and it's also Fashion Week..."

"Oooh! That's nice!"

"The other 21 days are floating days – I can split them into studio or 1 bedroom which gives me a total of up to 49 days to stay here and use the amenities and if I don't want to do that, I can exchange my week, I can put a week into their rental program, or I can convert them to Marriott Bonvoy Platinum Level points to stay at one of their resorts..."

"Oh wow! I had no idea you could do this in real estate!"

"We found out early..."

"Early?"

"These opportunities don't come along often – when you find an opportunity to own a piece of real estate in New York – even if it's a Deeded Fractional Share – it's a win-win – you'll own a huge piece of a rich pie..."

"So that's why they call New York the Big Apple!" I laughed...

"I knew you'd get it..." he breathed as he pulled me into a kiss. Darnell pushed his tongue in my mouth, pushed me down on my back, and we couldn't control ourselves...

"Mmmph... Mmmph... Mmmph..." Darnell slid his hand in my pants and when he felt how wet I was he jumped up off me...

"What's wrong?" I exclaimed...

"Get up..." he commanded. I got up, stood in front of him, and looked at him...

"I'm going to show you around..." he breathed as he pulled me into a kiss...

"Mmm Hmmm..."

"And after I show you around... I'm going to take you into the master bedroom..." he breathed and then he kissed me again...

"Mmm Hmmm..."

"And then I'm going to undress you..." he breathed as he kissed me again...

"Mmm Hmmm..."

"And I'm going to go between your legs..." he breathed as he kissed me again...

"Mmm Hmmm..."

"And I'm going to taste you..." he breathed as he kissed me hard...

"Mmmmmm..." I moaned...

"This is the living room..."

"Okay..." I breathed...

"That's the first bedroom over there behind the French doors..." he said as he took my hand and led me over to the French doors...

"Oh wow..." I whispered. The room was decorated exactly as you'd expect in the St. Regis Hotel...

"This is one of the bathrooms..." he said as he took me into the first bathroom. As soon as I saw the Jacuzzi and the two sinks, something came over me and I got sad...

"It's nice..."

"This is the second bathroom..." he said as he led me into the second bathroom...

"This is nice too..."

"And now..." he said as he led me into the master bedroom... "I'm going to take your clothes off..." he breathed as he pushed my coat off my shoulders...

"Darnell... Stop..."

"You want me to stop?! Why?!"

"I'm sorry Darnell – I can't do this..." I whispered as I began to tear up...

"It's okay – we don't have to..." he said as he picked up my coat..."

"Could you take me home?"

"If that's what you want..." he sighed...

"I'm sorry Darnell..."

"So am I..." he sighed as he helped me put my coat on. We walked out into the living room and he opened the door for me. I walked out and Darnell closed the door behind us. I wanted to take his hand but I hesitated. He took my hand and I was relieved as we walked to the elevator.

Darnell tried his best to stay positive but I could see how hurt he was and I felt bad...

"Can we walk to Grand Central?"

"You sure you wanna walk?"

"Yea..."

"Okay..." he sighed as he took my hand and we began to walk towards Grand Central. We didn't speak for about 30 minutes...

"What time is the next train?" I asked...

"We can get the 2:47 on track 30 or we can get the 2:53 on track 40 – the 2:54 is on track 29..."

"Let's get the 2:53 on track 40..." I said as I took him by the hand and pulled him towards track 40...

"Whew – we made it..." I exclaimed as we got to track 40...

"Yes we did..." Darnell agreed. We got on the train, Darnell picked a seat, and we sat down...

"What are you doing?" I asked when I saw him take out his phone...

"I'm paying for the tickets – where do you live?"

"You're not paying for the tickets – I am..." I said as I took out my phone and bought the tickets...

"You didn't have to do that..."

"I wanted to..." Darnell didn't say anything else. I was happy when he let me snuggle up underneath him and he put his arm around me again...

"Tickets please..." the conductor commanded. I took my phone out, activated the tickets, and showed him the phone...

"Thank you..." The 2:45 was a local train so I got comfortable and looked out the window as we stopped at Melrose, Tremont, Fordham, Botanical Garden, Williams Bridge, Woodburn, Wakefield, Mt. Vernon West, Fleetwood, Bronxville, Tuckahoe, Crestwood, Scarsdale, and Hartsdale...

"We're getting off at the next stop..." I said as I sat up...

"Okay..." Darnell sighed...

"White Plains..." We got up, got off the train, went inside, and got on the elevator. I wanted to kiss Darnell so bad but I knew he was still upset so I moved closer to him and took his hand. When we got downstairs and the doors opened, he spoke...

"Where are we going?"

"I'm taking you home with me..."

"You live here in White Plains?"

"Yes..."

"Hmmm – I didn't know that..." he said as he smiled. I was relieved and turned on...

"Isn't this the Opus?"

"Yes..."

"Oh my God – you live here?!"

"Good afternoon Ms. Robinson..." the doorman greeted...

"Good afternoon Robert..." I greeted as I led Darnell into the lobby. Darnell was beaming as we went towards the elevator...

"I can't believe you live here..." he sighed...

"I've lived here for a little over 12 years and I still can't believe it..." I wanted to kiss him so bad but I fought the urge... "This is my Villa..." I said when we got to my door. I unlocked the door and Darnell followed me inside... "The coat closet is here – hang up your coat and make yourself comfortable..." I said as I hung up my coat. Darnell hung up his coat and followed me into the living room... "Would you like something to drink?"

"No – actually – I need to use the bathroom...

"The guest bath is right over there..." I said as I pointed towards the half-bath...

"Thanks..." he said as he got up and went to the bathroom. He was surprised when he opened the door and I was standing there... "Why are you standing here?" he laughed...

"I wanted to show you around..."

"Okay..."

"This is the guest room..." I said as I took his hand and led him into the guest room... "I'm using this as an office..."

"I can see that..." he said as he looked around...

"Go look in the bathroom..."

"Okay..." he said as he shrugged his shoulders and went to look in the bathroom... "Oh my God! This is nice! This walk in shower is big enough for two!"

"I know..." I said as I walked into the bathroom. Darnell looked back at me and I smiled at him mischievously... "C'mon – I'll show you the master bath..." I said as I took his hand and led him through the living room, past the kitchen, and into the master bathroom...

"Wow! Look at that soaker tub! It's huge! This bathroom is the size of another bedroom!"

"I know..."

"And that mirror behind the tub... wow..."

"The walk-in shower is over there..." I said as I pointed towards the shower. Darnell looked over at the shower, walked over to me, and pulled me into a kiss...

"Where's the master bedroom?"

"It's... behind... you..." I breathed. Darnell turned around, took me by the hand, and led me into the master bedroom...

"Oh wow..."

"This is my favorite room..."

"I can see why..."

"I have a wall of closet space and a walk in closet..."

"You have a king-sized bed..."

"It's my first one..."

"Is that right?"

"Yea..."

"Why?"

"I've never had a place big enough to have a king-sized bed..."

"So..." Darnell said as he walked over to me... "Do you close the shade when you get undressed?" he asked as he began to walk me back towards the bed...

"No..." Darnell stood in front of me, breathing heavily, waiting for me to give him permission to do what he wanted to do. He didn't have to wait long...

"Taste me..." I breathed as I pulled him into a kiss. Darnell pushed me back on the bed and began to take off his clothes. I was breathing heavy as he tortured me with a slow strip-tease. He stood at the end of the bed and stared at me with his hands on his hips as I focused on his dick. Darnell climbed on the bed, spread my legs, got between them, and pulled me up by my arms...

"Put your arms up..." he commanded. I did as I was told and he pulled my blouse up over my head. I put my arms down and he pushed me back down on my back. He began kissing me, pushed his tongue in my mouth, slid his arms up

23

under me, unclasped my bra, and pushed it down off my shoulders as we continued kissing. Now that my bra was off, he began squeezing my breasts in his hands as he kissed my neck...

"Ooohhh..." I moaned. Darnell kissed his way down my body and took my left breast in his mouth first... "Ooohhh... Darnell..." I moaned as he sucked hungrily while continuing to squeeze my right breast. He moved over to my left breast and began sucking on it as he squeezed my right breast... "Darnell... Darnell..." I moaned as I arched my back. Darnell kissed his way down my body and when he got to my belly button, he opened my pants and slid them off my hips along with my panties. Once he got them off my legs he spoke...

"Spread your legs..." he commanded. I spread my legs, he grabbed my ass in his hands, and dove in...

"Darnell!" I moaned as I arched my back. Darnell slid his hands up under me further and slid his tongue inside me... "Oh Darnell... Huh..." I moaned as he devoured me. It was as if this was his first time and he was savoring every bit of my thirst-quenching as I squirted uncontrollably...

"Damn..." he breathed and then he put his tongue back inside me and swirled it around...

"Darnell... Darnell... Darnell..." He was relentless as he slid his tongue up, down, and around my clit... "Haa... Haa... Haa... Don't stop... Don't stop... I'm cumming... I'm..."

I was startled when he stopped but before I could react, he got up and thrust himself inside me as he held himself up on his arms...

"FUCK ME!!" I screamed as he continued thrusting. I wrapped my legs around him and he put his arms up under my back, pulled me close, and began pounding my pussy... "AAAHHH! YEESS!! FUCK ME!! DON'T STOP!!

"UUUGH!! UUUGH!! UUUGH!! UUUGH!! UUUGGGHHH!!" Darnell continued to hold me and when he kissed me hard, I began to cry... "Are you okay?" he whispered as he kissed my tears...

"I love you Darnell..."

"I love you too..." he breathed as he teared up and kissed me hard. I pushed my tongue in his mouth and he understood the assignment as he sucked my tongue and I started squirming... "Mmm..." he moaned in my mouth as he pushed his tongue in my mouth, grabbed my legs by my hips, and began pounding my pussy again...

"Mmmph... Mmmph... Mmmph..."
"Mmmm... Mmmm... Mmmm... Mmmm..."
"Mmmph... Mmmph... Mmmph..."
"Mmmm... Mmmm... Mmmm... Mmmm..."
"Mmmph... Mmmph... Mmmph..."
"Mmmm... Mmmm... Mmmm... Mmmm..."
"Mmmph... Mmmph... Mmmph..."
"Mmmm... Mmmm... Mmmm... Mmmm..."
"MMMPH!! MMMPH!! MMMPH!!"
"MMMM!! MMMM!! MMMM!! MMMM!!"

We continued kissing and crying for a few moments and then I spoke...
"I need to tell you something..."
"Okay..." he breathed...
"You're the only man that's ever been here..."
"Are you serious?"
"Yes..."
"Damn..." he breathed as he kissed me again. We continued kissing and when I left his tears on my face, I started crying again too... "Marry me..."
"What did you say?" I breathed...
"I said Marry me..."
"Yes..."

"What did you say?" he asked as if he didn't hear me...

"I said yes..."

"Say it again..." he breathed as he started thrusting...

"Yeeesss..." I moaned...

"Again..." he grunted...

"Yeeesss..." I moaned...

"AGAIN!!" he commanded as he began fucking me harder...

"YEESSS!!"

"AGAIN!!" he growled as he pounded...

"YEESSS!!" I moaned as I came again...

"UUUGGGHHH!!" Darnell collapsed on top of me and we both fell asleep...

"Ouch..."

"Ouch?!" Darnell exclaimed as he jumped up... "What's wrong?"

"I'm in pain..." I answered as I pushed myself up...

"In pain?! Where?!"

"Here..." I answered as I took his hand and put it on my right side...

"Is it my fault?" he asked out of concern...

"I don't think so..."

"So... It could be my fault?"

"Well..."

"Oh my God – I'm sorry – I didn't mean to hurt you..."

"Yes you did!" I laughed...

"Chelle! Don't say that!"

"Darnell – What did I tell you to do?" he didn't answer me right away...

"Umm... You told me to taste you..."

"And what else did I tell you to do?"

"Well... Ummm... You told me to fuck you..."

"Did you want to?"

"Hell yea I wanted to!"

"And I wanted you to..."

"Can you get up?"

"I can try..." I answered as I tried again and failed... "Ouch!"

"Okay – that's it!" he exclaimed as he jumped up and hurried into the bathroom. I realized what he was doing when I heard the water running... "I'm going to put you in the tub..." he explained as he came back in the room, came over to the side of the bed, and picked me up in his arms. I put my arms around his neck and he carried me into the bathroom... "I'm going to sit you on the side of the tub, I'll get in, and then I'll help you in – okay?"

"Okay." Darnell didn't put me down right away. He looked in the mirror as he held me for a few moments and then he put me down... "This is a first..."

"A first?"

"This is the first time I'm going to be taking a bath with my man..."

"Your husband..." he corrected as he sat down in the water. Darnell helped me into the water and I was on his lap... "Lay back..." he commanded. I laid back on his chest and he began to massage my body under the water...

"Ooohhh... That feels good..."

"Close your eyes..." he commanded. I closed my eyes and he continued to massage me. When he moved his hands up to my breasts, I spoke...

"They don't hurt..."

"Ssshhh..." he whispered as he continued to massage them. He knew I was turned on when my nipples got hard... "You like this..."

"Yeess..." I breathed...

"Keep your eyes closed..." he whispered as he continued to massage them and squeeze them. I put my hands over his as he continued. He moved our hands down to my waist and began massaging my waist on both sides...

"Ooohhh..." I moaned...

"Keep your eyes closed... Relax..." he whispered. He moved his hands to my stomach and massaged me from my stomach to my waist and back to my stomach again... "How does that feel?" he whispered...

"It... feels... good..." I breathed...

"Keep your eyes closed..." he whispered as he moved one hand up to my right breast and the other between my legs...

"Oh Darnell..." I moaned...

"Keep your eyes closed..." he whispered as he began swirling his fingers around my clit...

"Oh... Oh... Oh..." I moaned. Darnell continued to massage my right breast as he swirled his fingers around my clit a bit harder...

"Oh Darnell... Darnell..." I moaned...

"Spread your legs... and keep your eyes closed..." he whispered. I did as I was told and he pushed his dick up inside me...

"Oh Darnell..." I moaned...

"Keep your eyes closed..." he whispered as he moved his hands down to my waist and moved me back and forth...

"Oh Darnell... Yeesss..." I moaned as I rode his dick backwards in the water. Darnell pushed himself up inside me deeper and hit my spot... "Huh... Darnell... Fuck..."

"Keep your eyes closed..." he whispered as he continued pushing my waist back and forth...

"I'm cumming..."

"Cum for me..."

"Huh... Huh... Huh... Huh... HHUUUHHH!!" Darnell pulled his dick out of me and I thought we were finished...

"Keep your eyes closed... and don't move..." he growled in my ear as he began to beat his dick against my clit...

"Oh Darnell... Yeesss..." I moaned. I reached under the water, grabbed his dick, and rubbed it against my clit hard...

"Oh shit... that's it... right there..." he breathed in my ear...

"Oh fuck... I'm cumming again..."

"I'm cumming with you..."

"Aah... Aah... Aah... Aah..."

"I'm cumming... Uuugghhh!!" I opened my eyes and looked at his cum floating in the water...

"Another first..." I breathed...

"You've never done that before?"

"Never..."

"How do you feel?"

"I feel good..." I breathed...

"Are you still in pain?" he asked as he pushed down on my side...

"A little..."

"I'll help you up...." he said as he stood up... "Give me your hands..." I gave him my hands, he braced himself against the wall, and pulled me up into his arms...

"I can't wait to celebrate our anniversary..." I breathed...

"You're already looking forward to our anniversary?"

"Yes..."

"That's sweet..." he breathed as he kissed me...

"I want you to tell me to marry you again and when I say yes, I want you to tell me say it again, fuck me, tell me say it again, fuck me, tell me to say it again, and fuck me again..."

"I can do that..."

"And if I need to soak in the tub again, we can do that too..."

"Do we have to wait for our anniversary for that?" he breathed as he pulled me into a kiss...

"No..."

"Good..." he breathed as he got out the tub...

"Where are you going?"

"I'll be right back..." I stood there and waited for him to come back and he had body wash in one hand the loofah in the other. I smiled at him as he got back in the tub. He dipped the loofah in the water, lathered it up good, and began washing me...

"That tickles!" I laughed...

"I'll be quick..." he said as he washed me all over. After he rinsed me off he sat down on the side of the tub, grabbed my ass, and pushed my pussy towards his face...

"Darnell..." I moaned as he spread my lips with his tongue... "Oh Darnell... Huh..." I moaned as I grabbed his head on both sides and held him in place...

"Mmmph... Mmmph... Mmmph..."

"Darnell... I'm cumming... I'm cumming... Aaahhh!" Darnell continued licking and sucking softly as I shook from the mini-gasms and then he moved his hands....

"I'm weak..." I panted...

"Maybe you should sit down..."

"I will in a minute..." I said as I took the loofah, lathered it up, and began to wash him...

"That feels nice..." he breathed. I took my time, washing in circular motions, massaging his body as I moved the loofah along his body. When I got to his ass he tensed up... "What are you doing?"

"I won't do anything you don't want me to do..." I breathed as I began kissing him on his ass...

"It does feel nice..."

"Good..." I breathed as I kissed his ass all over. I didn't spread his cheeks and I knew he was relieved but I also knew he wasn't prepared for what happened next...

"Chelle! Oh shit!" he moaned as I grabbed his ass and pushed his dick in my mouth... "Oh... Fuck..." he moaned as I swirled my tongue around the head of his dick. Darnell let me take complete control as I pushed him in slowly and he became concerned when I gagged... "Are you okay?" he whispered. I didn't answer him – I just relaxed my throat and pushed him in until my lips were touching his balls... "FFFUUUCCCKKK!!" he growled as he grabbed my head on both sides and came in my mouth. I swallowed immediately and continued sucking softly as I eased my mouth off his dick... "Damn Baby..." he panted as he leaned back against the wall...

"I wasn't sure I could do that..." I breathed...

"You're the first..."

"I am?!" I exclaimed...

"Yes..." I stood up and gave myself a pat on my back... "C'mon – let's get outta here – I'm hungry..." he said as he stepped out the tub...

"Your bathrobe is right there..." I said as I pointed to the robe labeled 'HIS'...

"Is this new?"

"Yes..."

"You bought this for me?"

"Yes..."

"Darnell started to tear up...

"What's wrong?"

"Nothing..." he sighed as he helped me out of the tub, I put my robe on, and we went into the kitchen...

"Let's see what you have in here..." Darnell said as he looked in the freezer... "Hmmm – you have chicken – I'll start with that..." he said as he put the chicken in the sink and filled it with water... "Oh nice – you have Jasmine rice..." he said as he put that on the counter...

"You like Jasmine rice?"

"I love it..." he answered as he went back into the refrigerator... "You want string beans or collard greens?"

"String beans..."

"Okay – I see you have some chicken broth in here too – that'll work..." he said as he took that out the refrigerator...

"I also have wine..."

"Red or white?"

"I have white moscato..."

"In here?" he asked as he pointed to the refrigerator...

"In the wine fridge..."

"The wine fridge?"

"In the island..."

"Oh! Okay!" he exclaimed as he took out a bottle of moscato...

"What's your drink of choice?"

"I like a good bourbon..."

"I'm surprised you didn't say Henney..."

"Why – because I'm Black?" We both bust out laughing...

"Aaa Haaa Haaa Haaa!"

"I deserved that..."

"It's okay – but everybody thinks all Black men drink Henney – I'm a bourbon man..."

"Let me know which one you want and I'll have it here for you..."

"Damn I love you..." he sighed as he poured me a glass of wine...

"I love you too..."

"I guess I'll have some wine with you..." he said as he took out a glass...

"Wait a minute..." I said as I got up and went over to the intercom...

"Good evening Ms. Robinson..."

"Good evening Robert – could you do me a favor?"

"What can I do for you?"

"Could you go to Kanopi and see if they have bourbon on the menu?"

"Sure..."

"Thank you..."

"You didn't have to send the man out to the liquor store!" Darnell exclaimed...

"I didn't send him to the liquor store..." I laughed... "I sent him to the restaurant..."

"The restaurant?"

"We have a restaurant downstairs..."

"In the building?"

"Yes..."

"Oh shit!"

"I go in there every so often..."

"Damn – I wish I had a restaurant in my building to go to when I didn't feel like cooking!" he exclaimed as we heard a knock at the door...

"Who is it?"

"It's Robert Maam..." Darnell hid as I answered the door...

"I'm sorry Ms. Robinson – I asked the manager – he said the closest drink they had to bourbon was the Zorro's Daiquiri – it's made with Golden Rum, Sugar, and Lime – if you like it you can stop by tomorrow and pay him...

"Darnell?"

"Yes Chelle?" he beamed as he came to the door...

"This is a Zorro's Daiquiri – it's made with Golden Run, Sugar, and Lime – let me know what you think..."

"Here you go sir..." Robert said as he handed Darnell the glass...

"Oh shit! This is good! Thank you!"

"You're welcome..." I said...

"I'm glad you like it Maam..."

"Robert – please don't call me Maam..."

"Ms. Robinson..."

"That's better..."

"Would you like me to bring you another drink Sir?"

"No... No thank you..."

"Very well... enjoy your night..." Robert said as he walked to the elevator...

"Damn! I'm hatin' big time right now!"

"He gets paid out of our HOA feels..."

"I bet the fees are high..." he said as he handed me the glass of moscato and finished his drink. I sat at the island and watched him intently as he began cooking...

"They're high..." I sighed...

"I can imagine how hi they are – especially with a mortgage..."

"I don't have a mortgage..."

"What?! I mean – that's great!"

"It sure is..."

"How'd you do it?"

"I started working when I was 18. I worked a main job, a second job, and a third job..."

"You worked three jobs?!"

"I did..."

"When did you sleep?!"

"I slept when I got home..."

39

"What time did you get home?!"

"I always got home between 10 and 12..."

"Midnight?!"

"Yes..."

"How long did it take you?"

"It took me 10 years..."

"Wow! That's amazing!"

"I had a one-bedroom at Rockledge but I've always wanted to live in the Opus since it was called the Ritz..."

"I remember that!"

"I lucked up on this condo..."

"How?"

"I came to an open house here and the owner was in a hurry to get out at the time..."

"That's good..."

"It certainly was – the owner was only asking $749..."

"For this?!"

"Yup..."

"Wow!"

"I sold my one-bedroom and that covered the down payment and closing costs..."

"How did you get approved for a mortgage?"

"I showed them all my tax returns and instead of putting down twenty percent I put down forty five percent..."

"Oh shit!"

"I wasn't playing! Thank God my condo sold for over asking or I would've been looking for another one-bedroom!"

"I'm so proud of you!"

"I paid my monthly fees every month, I paid on the principle every time I got paid from the second job, and I applied my tax refund to the principle every year – for 10 years!"

"You said you had a third job..."

"I worked on Saturday and Sunday – I used that money to go out on Fridays – that was my only day off..."

"I'm so proud of you!"

"Thank you... I'm proud of myself..."

"I can't believe you own this!"

"I lucked up and got this for $749 – and now it's worth $1.5..."

"Oh shit! Yeesss!"

"My HOA fees and taxes are $2269 – if my mortgage wasn't paid off my monthly payment would be over $5k..."

"I'm so proud of you!"

"I was so happy when I was finally able to quit my other jobs – I ran around in here naked shouting thank you Jesus every day for two weeks!!"

"Thank you Jesus!" Darnell exclaimed. I looked at him and I knew he meant it...

"Does anybody else know?!"

"My best friend..."

"That's it?! Nobody else?!"

"Well – you know now..."

"Why'd you tell me?"

"You're going to be my husband – I trust you...

"I love you..." he said as he put the plates on the island...

"I love you too..." I said as he took my hands...

"Thank you Jesus..." he said as he teared up...

"Thank you Jesus..." I sighed...

"I was so mad that day when my Uber was cancelled..."

"I know..."

"I should've known that was God..."

"That was God..." I sighed...

"You pulled up at that light... and my life is so much better now... Thank you Jesus..." he said again as he started crying...

"Thank you Jesus..." I sighed as I started crying too...

"Let's eat – I wanna know what you think of my cooking..."

"If it tastes as good as it smells, I think I'll love it..." I said as I cut the chicken and took a bite... "Oh my God – this is so good..."

"I'm glad you like it..."

"I'm glad you can cook..." I laughed as we ate...

Darnell put the dishes in the dishwasher and came to sit beside me on the couch...

"We need to talk..." I sighed...

"About?"

"About earlier..."

"I really enjoyed earlier..." he breathed as he kissed me...

"I mean earlier..."

"Ohhh..." he sighed as he sat back and looked at me...

"I've been keeping something from you..."

"What could you possibly be keeping from me?"

"Before we met, I scheduled my vacation six weeks in advance..."

"Okay..."

"I went into work on Friday and before I could finish my coffee, my director told me she wasn't approving my vacation..."

"On your last day?!"

"Yes..."

"Fuckin' Bitch!"

"That's what I thought too..."

"So you went anyway..."

"Yes..."

"I'm surprised you got away with that..."

"That was definitely God..."

"What happened?"

"I emailed Victoria in personnel..."

"Victoria? At 112?"

"Yes..."

"Okay..."

"I forwarded the email I got that said my vacation wasn't approved and I added that my director told me I needed to get a refund or a credit because she wasn't approving my vacation..."

"Oh shit! She actually told you that?!"

"Yes – so I put that in the email – and I also said I was disheartened and it made me sad because I didn't feel like a valued employee..."

"Damn Chelle... I'm sorry..."

"So after I sent the email, my director demanded I come in her office and I told her I couldn't because I needed to finish my work before I go on vacation..."

"Was that true or you just said that because you didn't want to go in her office?"

"Both..."

"Okay..."

"So she gets up, comes behind me, and yells I SAID I NEED TO SEE YOU IN MY OFFICE – NOW!!"

"What?!"

"I've only been spoken to one other time like that at work – and I went home crying..."

"I'm so sorry..." he said as he took my hand... "What did you do?"

"Everyone was watching me... I was so mad I was shaking... so I called Victoria and left a message saying that my director was yelling at me, she was being hostile, and I was leaving for the day because I felt threatened..."

"Did you really feel threatened?"

"Yes..."

"This director must be a piece of work..."

"She was..."

"Was?"

"I left for the day and after I had lunch, Victoria called me..."

"Oh no..."

"I was worried too until she told me she had good news..."

"Good news?"

"I put in a request to be transferred and it was approved..."

"Wait a minute – how long did you put in a request for a transfer?"

"About two months ago..."

"So you wanted out before you put in your request for vacation..."

"Yes..."

"When did you start at 85?"

"January 4th..."

"Where did you work before that?"

"112..." Darnell sat there for a few moments thinking and by the look on his face, I knew he had put it together...

"You worked for my wife – right?"

"Yes..." I answered as I started crying...

"So... All this time..."

"No Darnell..."

"So... You didn't know Dana was my wife?"

"Not at first..."

"Not at first?! What does that mean?!"

"I didn't know Dana was your wife until we got back to the airport..."

"The airport?!"

"When they said they needed to speak to you about your wife, I heard you say Dana..."

"So... I mourned my wife... I felt guilty about being with you when she died... I planned her funeral... I buried her... And you never said anything – why?!"

"I didn't want to lose you..." I whispered...

"You really love me..." he whispered as he teared up...

"Yes..."

"I don't understand... What does this have to do with what happened earlier?"

"When you took me into the master bathroom... I started thinking about her... and when you took me in the bedroom... all I could think about was you in bed with her... I started feeling like I was your mistress... I just couldn't do it..."

"Oh my God..." he whispered as he pulled me into his arms and held me...

"I'm sorry – I know she's dead but..."

"Baby... No..." he breathed as he kissed me... "If I had known – I never would've taken you there – I wanted to surprise you..."

"And I ruined it..."

"I thought you didn't want me..." he whispered as tears fell down his cheeks...

"It was so hard to stay away from you while you were making her arrangements..."

"You wanted me then?"

"I've wanted you ever since I felt your breath on my hand..."

"When I kissed your hand in the Uber?"

"Yes..."

"I thought what happened between us in Bermuda was going to stay in Bermuda..."

"I knew that wasn't happening when you kissed me at the airport..."

"I kissed you three times at the airport..."

"I couldn't wait to get to Bermuda and let you make love to me – especially after I went to get us coffee..."

"What happened when you went to get us coffee?!"

"The cashier told me you were my husband..."

"How could she know that?!"

"She said she saw you propose to me..." Darnell sat there and smiled. He knew what that smile did to me...

"So..." he breathed as he pulled me into a kiss, pushed me down on the couch, laid on top of me, and opened my robe... "If she saw me propose to you..." he breathed in my ear... "She must've seen me fucking you..." he breathed as he eased himself inside me...

"Oh Darnell... Yeessss..."

"Darnell..."

"Hmmm?"

"C'mon..." I sighed as I stood up...

"Where are we going?"

"To bed..." I yawned...

"Okay..." he yawned as he got up and stretched. Darnell followed me into the bedroom and got in the bed before I could...

"You must be tired..." I laughed as I got in bed and snuggled up next to him...

"I haven't fucked this much in one day since I was in my twenties..."

"Get used it it..." I laughed...

"It's like that?!"

"I'm in my thirties – you're in your forties – you're about to turn up..."

"I am?!"

"Oh yea..."

"Okay!"

"I turn up again in my fifties when you start to wind down in your sixties..."

"That's fucked up..."

"I'm not worried about it..."

"You're not?"

"Naa... My pussy will call you – and you'll answer..."

"Oh shit!"

"I need to ask you something..."

"Okay..."

"Do you want children?" Darnell didn't answer me right away...

"I need to tell you something..."

"Okay..."

"I had a vasectomy a few years ago..."

"You never wanted children?"

"No..."

"Why?"

"It's not that I don't like kids – I love kids – I've just always wanted to do me..."

"I guess that wasn't a problem for Dana..."

"What makes you say that?"

"She was older – I know she didn't want any more children..."

"No she didn't – but let's talk about you – do you want children?"

"I did..."

"I'm sorry..."

"I'm not..."

"You're not?"

"Hell no – I can get this depo outta me – I've been on birth control for the last 10 years – I can't wait to fuck as much as I want without getting pregnant!"

"Alrighty then!" he laughed...

"I want to go back to your condo at St. Regis..."

"Are you sure?"

"When was the last time the mattresses were changed?"

"You know what – that's a good question!"

"Let's put new mattresses in there – and as soon as they get delivered I want to be the first one to get fucked on them!"

"Okay!"

"I love you Mr. Tompkins..."

"I love you too Mrs. Tompkins..."

"This is going to be so weird..."

"Weird?"

"Yes – especially when we go see Victoria in personnel..."

"Why do we need to go see Victoria in personnel?"

"We need to fill out our paperwork, change beneficiaries, and I need to change my name..."

"You really want to do that?"

"Hell yea!!"

"You know people are gonna talk..."

"People have been talking..."

"About me?"

"Well..."

"What did you hear?" he asked as he propped himself up on his elbow...

"People were talking about your wife... and Kevin..."

"People know?!"

"Nobody knew for sure – but people used to talk about how Dana would always be in Kevin's office after hours with the door closed..."

"Fuckin' Bitch..."

"They talked about Tracy too..."

"Tracy? Tracy who?"

"Jeruh's secretary..."

"Oh shit! He was fuckin' her?!"

"No – it wasn't like that – she just spent a lot of time in his office because she looked up to him..."

"Are you sure about that?"

"Oh yea – Jeruh was nice to all the secretaries – he saw me in the deli one day and he told the cashier I'm paying for all their coffee – and her's too!" I laughed...

"Damn – he didn't even know your name!"

"Nope – even when they had parties he'd walk around and invite all the secretaries – he'd say make sure you invite her, her, and her too..."

'I'm glad he was nice..."

"He was..."

"You know they're gonna talk about us – right?" I propped myself up on my elbow and kissed him...

"I don't give a fuck what anybody says about me and my husband..."

"Neither do I..." he breathed as he kissed me back... "But I do need to tell you something...

"Okay..."

"When I told my wife I wanted a divorce, it was uncontested – I didn't want anything..."

"Ohhh..."

"Since we were still married when she died, I got her life insurance, her 401k, and her pension..."

"Oh wow..."

"I get $6k a month from her..."

"Oh my God!"

"She was 10 years older than me – she was about to retire..."

"Oh yea – that's right..."

"I don't know if I can add you as a beneficiary to any of that..."

"Darnell – I don't care about that – I thought you'd be divorced – I expected your wife to be alive..."

"So did I..."

"Besides – I can add you as my beneficiary..."

"I can add you as my beneficiary on my bank accounts, my life insurance, and my pension..."

"Hmmm..."

"What are you thinking?"

"It's a good thing you can collect her pension and still work for New York State..."

"That's because it's her pension – not my pension...

"And since you're going to make me the beneficiary on your bank accounts... and your money goes into those accounts..."

"Le'me find out you want me for my money!" he laughed...

"That's not what I'm saying!" I laughed...

"What are you saying then?"

"I was going to say I think we should keep our accounts separate..."

"Even after we're married?"

"Yea..."

"Okay..."

"I'm the beneficiary on yours – and you're the beneficiary on mine – I'll just change my name to my married name..."

"Okay so let me get this straight – we're going to personnel – you're my beneficiary – I'm your beneficiary – you're changing your name – and the accounts stay as they are – except we add each other as beneficiaries..."

"Yes..."

"I have something else I need to tell you..."

"Okay..."

"Dana had a three-bedroom condo on Davenport Avenue in New Roc City..."

"Had?"

"Well – it's mine now..."

"I'll never live there..."

"Understood..."

"Do you wanna keep it?"

"I'll sell it..." he sighed...

"I'm sorry..."

"I don't need to keep it – especially since you said you'll never live there..."

"I won't..."

"Okay – I heard you..."

"I have an idea..."

"I'm listening..."

"Why don't you sell that one in New Roc... and buy one here?"

"In the Opus?"

"Yes..."

"Will you sell yours?"

"I worked so hard to pay this off..."

"I know..."

"It's the only thing I have that's all mine..."

"I understand... It's just that Dana still has a mortgage on that property – her pension and 401k was going to be used to make the payments so... I was thinking I could use her money to pay the mortgage and HOA fees and you could move in with me..."

"I'm sorry... It would be different if I didn't know her... but I did know her... and I don't like New Rochelle..."

"You don't like New Rochelle?"

"The only thing I like in New Rochelle is the country clubs..."

"That's it?"

"I love it here – I'm in walking distance to everything – restaurants – pharmacies – banks – doctors – my job..."

"Okay – how 'bout this?"

"I'm listening..."

"I'll sell it..."

"Okay..."

"I'll buy another one here..."

"Okay..."

"You'll move in with me..."

"Umm..."

"Hear me out..."

"Okay..."

"You keep yours for as long as you want..."

"Okay..."

"And I'll keep mine at St. Regis..."

"Okay..." I sighed...

"Are you sure you're okay with this?"

"Well..."

"Chelle... Talk to me..."

"Okay... So there are a few 3 bedrooms available in this building and in the building next to us... but my favorite is the penthouse in this building at 3EFG..."

"EFG?"

"It's 4 bedrooms, 4.5 baths, 5079 square feet..."

"And you'd buy that if you could?"

"Yes..."

"How much are the monthly payments?"

"Well..."

"How much?"

"A little over... $10,000..."

"A month?!"

"Yes..."

"How are you going to afford that?"

"I was going to use the money from the jackpot..."

"Jackpot?! You mean Powerball?!"

"Powerball or Mega..." I sighed...

"Okay – let's be practical – what if you don't hit the jackpot?"

"Well... there's a 3 bedroom, 3.5 bath unit at 23C – the monthly payments are a little over $4,000 – but it's not my favorite..."

"Do you have another favorite? Like the one you can't afford?"

"Yes... but..."

"What's wrong?"

"It's in the building behind us..."

"Okay..."

"It's 4 bedrooms, 4.5 baths, and it's 3044 square feet..."

"Wow..."

"It's listed at $2.4..."

"Okay..."

"The payments are $5,532..."

"That's half of your favorite..."

"It's my 2nd favorite..."

"Do you have a 3rd?"

"Yes..."

"Tell me..."

"Well... there's a 4 bedroom, 4.5 bath unit at penthouse 8G, it has a built-in fireplace and the monthly payments are over $10,000..."

"I have a question for you..."

"Okay..."

"Do you think you could fall in love with your second choice if we could get it? Even though it doesn't have a fireplace?"

"Yes..."

"You said it was $2.4..."

"Yes..."

"Dana's condo is valued at $2,050,000..."

"Okay..."

"Yours is valued at $1.5..."

"Okay..."

"We could both sell our units and we'd have more than enough to buy the unit you like..."

"Okay..." I sighed as I smiled...

"I'll use Dana's money to pay the mortgage off..."

"Okay..."

"My payments are $2972 – your payments are $2269 – that's $5241 – I'll put in the difference and we can get the 3 bedroom..."

"Okay – I'll do it –however..."

"Talk to me..."

"You sell your condo first..."

"Okay..."

"You buy the 3 bedroom condo here..."

"Okay..."

"After we close, I'll move in with you and then I'll list mine..."

"So I'll be paying the mortgage and maintenance by myself until you sell your unit..."

"Yes..."

"I guess I can do that..."

"You don't trust me?"

"That's not it..."

"What is it then?"

"Can I move in here with you?"

"You want us to live together before we get married?"

"Yes..."

"I'm not going anywhere!" I laughed...

"I'm not worried about that – I'm worried about being homeless..."

"Ohhh..."

"I know Dana's condo will sell right away – I want to make sure I have somewhere to go when it sells..."

"You can move in with me..." I sighed as I kissed him...

"Good – now that we've settled that..." he breathed as he pushed me back down on the bed and got on top of me... "I need to set a few ground rules..."

"Ground rules?"

"Yes..."

"Okay..."

"For starters..." he breathed as he kissed me... You need to start closing these shades..."

"I do?"

"You do..."

"Okay... What else?"

"You need to let me taste you..." he breathed as he slid down between my legs...

"I... I can... do... that..." I panted...

"Good..." he breathed as he spread my lips with his tongue and began flicking it against my clit...

"What... What else?" I moaned...

"I'll let you know when I'm finished!" he growled as he dove in...

"Chelle..." Darnell whispered...

"Huh?" I yawned...

"Open your eyes..."

"My eyes are open..." I sighed...

"Okay – that's it – I need you to get up, put on your robe – and meet me in the kitchen..." he commanded as he walked out of the bedroom. I was wondering what was so urgent so I jumped up out the bed, put on my robe, and went to meet him in the kitchen...

"Oh Darnell..." I cried when I saw what was on the island. Darnell had a bottle of champagne, a single peach rose in a vase, two champagne flutes filled with champagne, and a small box in the middle of the island... "I'll be right back!" I exclaimed as I hurried into the office...

"What are you doing?!"

"I'll be right there!" I exclaimed as I dug in my purse, grabbed the box out the bottom, and shoved it into my robe pocket before he could catch me...

"Umm... you wanna tell me why you had to rush in here?"

"I thought I left my printer on..." I lied as I walked over to him. Darnell gave me the side eye and then he pulled me into a kiss... "I love you too..." I breathed. He hesitated for a second and then he led me into the kitchen...

"Have a seat..." he commanded...

"Okay..." Darnell waited for me to sit down and then he opened the box...

"I know I proposed to you earlier... but I wanted to make it official..." he said as he put the ring on my finger and I started crying... "Will you marry me Chelle?"

"Yes Darnell... Yes..." I cried. Darnell cried too as he pulled my face to his and kissed me hard... "Now that you've asked me to marry you, I need you to do something for me..." I said as I took the box out my robe pocket and put it on the island between us. Darnell's eyes got really wide when he saw the box. I opened the box, took out the ring, and looked him in his eyes... "Darnell... I breathed as I put the ring on his finger... "Will you marry me?"

"Yes Chelle! Yes!" he exclaimed as he pulled my face to his and kissed me hard again.

We were kissing so much we almost knocked the champagne over...

"Le'me move this bottle..." he laughed...

"Here's to us..." I sighed as I picked up my champagne flute...

"Here's to us..." he sighed as he picked up his champagne flute and we both gulped down the champagne...

"I love you so much..." he sighed...

"I love you more..."

"I have a question for you..." he said as he took my hand and led me into the living room. He sat down on the couch and I sat down beside him... "When did you buy this ring?"

"I bought it on January 4th..."

"You bought it the same day you went back to work?!"

"Yes..."

"You've been planning to propose to me since we got back..." he said as he started crying...

"I need to tell you something..." I sighed...

"What's wrong?"

"After we left the airport, I called Veronica..."

"So... you told her?"

"Yea..."

"You told her everything?"

"Yea..." I sighed... "Are you upset with me?"

"No... I just hope you can trust her..."

"I can..."

"Okay..."

"I told her you gave me the bracelet for Christmas..."

"You did?"

"Yea..."

"What's wrong Chelle?"

"She thought you bought the bracelet to give to someone..."

"She thought I bought the bracelet to give to the first woman to give me some pussy..."

"How'd you know?"

"You told her everything – right?"

"Yea..."

"So she figured since I was on my way to Bermuda like you were I must be full of shit..."

"I'm sorry..."

"She got in your head..."

"No she didn't..."

"If she didn't get in your head – why did you go to Kay Jewelers?"

"I wanted to prove her wrong..."

"So you believed me?"

"Yes..."

"Are you telling me the truth?"

"Yes Darnell..."

"Okay – what happened when you got to Kay Jewelers?"

"I talked to Cindy..."

"I didn't know you knew Cindy..."

"She remembered me..."

"Oh so you've been there before?"

"I went there to buy the tennis bracelet before I booked my flight to Bermuda..."

"Ohh – okay..."

"I picked out the ring for you after Cindy told me what you said..."

"Cindy told you what I said?"

"Yea – she told me you said you were going to give the bracelet to the woman that was your now and forever..." Darnell smiled as tears fell down his face...

"You love me..."

"Yes Darnell..." I breathed as I pulled him into a kiss... "I love you..."

"Did you tell Veronica what happened at Kay Jewelers?"

"Yea – but I didn't tell her I bought you a ring..."

"Why not?"

"I wanted to wait until we made it official..."

"Okay – now that it's official – I want you to call Veronica – tell her you won't be in to work tomorrow – and tell her why..."

"You want me to call Veronica and tell her you proposed?"

"That's your best friend – right?"

"Yea..."

"Well – don't you think your best friend will be happy for you?"

"She'll be happy for me..."

"Go ahead – call her – and put the phone on speaker..."

"Okay!" I exclaimed as I dialed her number...

"Hey Chelle!" Veronica exclaimed...

"Hey Veronica – I have you on speaker..."

"Okay..."

"Darnell's here..."

"Umm... Okay..."

"He wanted me to call you and give you the good news..."

"Good news?"

"We're getting married!"

"WHAT?! Are you crazy?!"

"Veronica!"

"Take me off the damn speaker!" I took her off the speaker and Darnell shook his head...

"You're off speaker..." I sighed...

"Have you lost your mind?!"

"No!"

"The man just buried his wife on Sunday – it's only Thursday – it hasn't even been a week yet – don't you think you should let his wife turn over in her grave before you get married?!"

"I guess you have a point..." I sighed...

"I'm sorry – I wish he wasn't there and I wish you didn't have me on speaker – but you knew I was gonna tell you the truth – right?"

"Yea..." I sighed...

"I'm not saying you can't marry him – I just think you should wait a while – you know when this gets out people are gonna talk..."

"They're gonna talk anyway..."

"I know that – but you don't want people calling you a homewrecker..."

"That's true..."

"You still taking tomorrow off?"

"Yea..."

"You know I love you – right?"

"I know..."

"Okay – I'll put you out for PL – I guess I'll see you on Tuesday..."

"See you Tuesday..." I sighed as I hung up. Darnell heard the conversation so he knew how I was feeling. He pulled me into a hug and held me...

"We can wait a while if you want..." he sighed...

"Why'd you want me to take the day off tomorrow?"

"Well... I was thinking we could go to city hall and apply for our marriage license..."

"Let's do it!"

"Are you sure?"

"Hell yea I'm sure!" I exclaimed as I called Veronica back...

"Yea Chelle..."

"I'm taking Tuesday off too..."

"You are? So you'll be back Wednesday?"

"Yea..."

"Okay – I'll see you Wednesday then!"

"Okay – bye!" I exclaimed as I hung up...

"What was that about?"

"I wanna get married!"

"Umm... okay..." he laughed...

"I wanna get our marriage license tomorrow – and I wanna get married on Tuesday!"

"What about what Veronica said?"

"What about it?"

"I thought you said she had a point?"

"She does – and it's been duly noted – but I don't wanna wait – if they're gonna talk about me – they're gonna talk about you being my husband!"

"Damn I love you..."

"I love you too – Let's go celebrate – I'm hungry!" I exclaimed as I jumped up and hurried into the bathroom...

"Good morning..." Darnell breathed as he kissed me awake...

"Good morning - let's go get our marriage license!" I exclaimed as I jumped up out of bed...

"Okay!" Darnell exclaimed as he jumped up off the bed and started getting dressed. We stopped to look at each other and he pulled me into a kiss... "Let's do this..." he breathed as he kissed me again...

"Mmmm.... Okay!" I exclaimed as I hurried up to get dressed and we both went out the door... "I can't believe we're actually doing this..."

"We are..."

"I can't wait to get to City hall..."

"Me either..." Darnell took my hand and we walked hand-in-hand to City Hall. When we went inside, we went straight to the City Clerk's office...

"Good morning – How may I help you?" Ms. Hurley asked...

"We're here to apply for our marriage license..." Darnell answered...

"Congratulations – do you have ID?"

"Yes we do..." Darnell answered as he put his ID on the counter and I added mine...

"Okay – here are your applications – fill them out, sign them, date them, give them to me, and I'll process them for you..."

"Okay..." Darnell said as he took the forms...

"Here Chelle – here's one for you..." he said as he pushed the form over to me and smiled...

"Darnell?"

"Yes Chelle?"

"I'm taking your name..."

"Really?"

"Yea..."

"I love you Chelle..."

"I love you too Darnell..."

"Keep your name too – especially since your property is in your maiden name..."

"I don't want to..."

"We're ready..." Darnell said as he took the papers from me and handed them to Ms. Hurley along with his papers...

"Okay – everything is in order – I just need to ask you both a few questions – I'll start with Chelle – is this your signature Chelle?"

"Yes…"

"Did you complete this application of your own free will?"

"Yes…" I answered as I smiled at Darnell…

"Okay – now that you've confirmed it's your signature and you've also confirmed that you completed this application of your own free will, I'll sign it…" Ms. Hurley said as she signed my application… "Okay Darnell – now it's your turn…" she said as she put his application in front of him… "Is this your signature?"

"Yes…"

"Did you complete this application of your own free will?"

"Yes I did…" Darnell answered as he smiled at me…

"Okay – now that you've confirmed it's your signature and you've also confirmed that you completed this application of your own free will, I'll sign it…" she said as she signed Darnell's application… "Wait here – I'm going to process the applications and I'll come back with your marriage license…" she said as she went to her office in the back…

"I'm so excited - I wish we could get married right now!" I exclaimed…

"You do?" Darnell asked…

"Yes…"

"Here's your marriage license…" Ms. Hurley said as she handed the marriage license to Darnell… "Do you have any questions?"

"How long do we have to wait before we can get married?"

"Are you in a hurry?" Ms. Hurley laughed…

"Yes I am…" I answered…

"Well… If you go to Connecticut, they don't impose a waiting period… so you can get married whenever you want – but here in New York you need to wait 48 hours…"

"Can we get married on Tuesday?"

"January 17th?"

"Yes…"

"Are you sure?" Darnell asked…

"Yes… I'm sure…"

"Okay – let me see what time we have available on Tuesday…" Ms. Hurley said as she opened the book…

"You can get married at 9 a.m. if that's not too early…"

"It's not too early!" I exclaimed…

"What she said!" Darnell laughed…

"Okay – I'll see you Tuesday morning at 9 a.m.…"

"Thank you Ms. Hurley!" I exclaimed as Darnell took me by the hand and pulled me outside…

"Where are we going?" I laughed…

"C'mon – I have something I want to show you – but we need to have breakfast first..." he answered as he pulled me down the ramp on to Main Street and we hurried down towards North Broadway. The only reason we stopped was because it was a green light – otherwise Darnell would've probably pulled me across the street. As soon as the light turned red, he took my hand and we crossed the street. I didn't question where we were going but when we started to go down the hill, I had an idea...

"We're going to the diner..." I sighed...

"Is that alright?"

"It's fine..." I sighed. We went inside and we were seated right away...

"Can I start you off with coffee?" the waitress asked...

"Yes please..." I answered...

"Coffee coming right up..." she said as she went to get the coffee...

"Have you eaten here before?" Darnell asked...

"Yes – but don't ask for turkey bacon – they give you Canadian bacon and think it's the same thing..."

"You don't like pork?"

"I do – but I love turkey bacon..." I answered as the waitress brought two cups over along with a pot of coffee and put them on the table...

"Are you ready to order?'

73

"I am – I'll have your hungry man special – scrambled with sausage, home fries, and pancakes..."

"You know what – I'll have that too..." Darnell said...

"That was easy..." the waitress said as she went to place our order...

"You must be really hungry!" he laughed as he started making his coffee...

"I hope they have hazelnut creamer..." I said as I looked through the bowl... "Found some! Yes!"

"So are you really hungry?"

"Huh?"

"Where are you?" Darnell laughed...

"I'm sorry – I'm so excited..."

"I'm excited too..."

"When we go back to work, we're going to be married!" Darnell didn't say anything – he just smiled at me as he sipped his coffee and I started sipping mine...

"Here ya go!" the waitress said as she put the food on the table...

"That was quick!" Darnell exclaimed...

"We aim to please – let me know if you need anything else..." she said as she walked away...

"This looks really good – I'm glad you ordered this..." he said as he went to take a bite...

"Thank you Jesus..." I sighed...

"Thank you Jesus..." he sighed. We didn't speak again until we were finished eating...

"Damn that was good!" I exclaimed...

"It sure was – we might have to come back here and get it again...

"I have another idea..."

"You do?"

"Yea – I want to take you to the Original Pancake House on Hamilton Avenue..."

"Is the food good?"

"It's slamming!" I answered as the waitress came over with the check...

"You ready?"

"I'm ready..."

"Let's do this then..." he said as he got up and I followed...

I was wondering why we were at the bus stop but I didn't question it. I was so happy I wasn't at work I didn't care why we were waiting for the bus. The bus pulled up and we got on. I didn't pay any attention to what bus it was but when we got off at Court Street and Martine Avenue I was curious...

"Where are we going now?"

"We're not going to work – don't worry!" he laughed as we got off the bus. As soon as I stepped off the bus I saw Ron...

"Good morning!" he exclaimed...

"Good morning..." I responded as cordial as I could muster...

"I guess I'll see you later..." he said as we walked off in the opposite direction...

"Veronica!" Ron exclaimed as he hurried inside...
"What?!"
"Guess who I just saw?"
"Who?"
"Chelle!"
"So!"
"She was with Dana's husband!"
"So!"
"Mmm!" he exclaimed as he went to sit down at his desk...

"We're getting on the 60..." Darnell said as the bus pulled up...
"Okay..." I sighed as I followed him on the bus. We went to sit down and he took my hand as I looked out the window...

I recognized where we were as soon as I saw North Avenue. I didn't say anything to Darnell though – I just got off the bus and when he took my hand, I let him lead me across the street. We waited for another bus and I noticed it was bus 45..."
"I used to take this bus all the time..." I said as I got on...
"You did? When?"
"When I went to Iona..."

"You graduated from Iona?"

"Yea..." Darnell smiled at me mischievously and we both knew what time it was. I was getting excited as we passed Iona College... "How much further?"

"Not much further..." he answered. I didn't ask him anymore questions. I continued to look out the window until we got to Davenport Avenue and then I smiled as I recognized where we were going...

"We're here..." he said as he got up. I got up, he took my hand, and we walked up to Watermark Pointe...

"Oh Darnell... it's beautiful!" I sighed...

"Wait 'till you see the inside..." he said as he took me into the building and we went to unit 2. Darnell unlocked the door and opened it for me... "Go ahead..." he said. I went inside and I was in awe. I still had the link in my phone from when we discussed selling his place but now that I was here, I realized the pictures didn't do his place justice...

"Oh Darnell..." I sighed. Darnell smiled at me as I walked around, taking in the panoramic views. The description was on point – this was definitely a resort inspired lifestyle. The unit was 3 bedrooms and designed with a contemporary feel and 10-inch ceilings. There was a private 30-foot terrace with unrestricted water views and the terrace had a gas barbeque grill. I went out on the deck and saw there was access to a private beach, a waterfront clubhouse, an outdoor heated pool overlooking the beach, and a fitness center. I went back inside and as I walked around, I realized some of the furniture wasn't something I would've picked out but that could easily be changed. I walked into the living room and I fell in love with the gas fireplace...

"This is nice..." I sighed. Darnell continued to smile at me and follow me as I went into the master bedroom and the master bath. I had to pee so I figured I might as well use the bathroom and when I was finished, I went to wash my hands and curiosity got the best of me so I opened the medicine cabinet. I saw two prescription bottles and I was even more curious... "What are you taking Darnell?" I whispered as I picked up the bottles, read them, and saw that they were prescribed to Dana... "Lithium, 600 milligrams, take twice a day with food – Risperdal, 3 milligrams – take once a day with food..." I had my phone with me so I went to google and pulled up the following information from the Mayo Clinic & Webb MD...

"Lithium is used to treat mania that is part of bipolar disorder (manic depressive illness)..."

"Risperdal is used to treat certain mental mood disorders such as schizophrenia and bipolar disorder. It works by helping to restore the balance of certain natural substances in the brain..."

I opened the bottles and dumped the medication in the toilet. I peeled the prescription information off both bottles, tore the papers into small pieces, threw them in the toilet, and flushed it. After I made sure everything went down, I threw the empty prescription bottles in the garbage. I came out the bathroom and went to look in the other bedrooms and bathrooms...

"Darnell – you can't sell this..."

"What did you just say?"

"You can't sell this..."

"But I thought..."

"Darnell..." I interrupted... "You wanted me to move in with you and now that I'm here... I can see why..."

"What are you saying?"

"I have a suggestion..."

"I'm listening..."

"What if we come here on the weekends and during the summer?"

"You mean... I don't have to sell it if I don't want to?"

"Yea..."

"Are you sure?"

"Yea..."

"I fuckin' love you!" he exclaimed as he picked me up off the floor, spun me around, and kissed me..."

"I fuckin' love you too!" I laughed as he put me down...

"You know..." he breathed in my ear... "We're not going back to work until Wednesday..."

"I know..." I laughed as he nibbled on my ear..."

"So... we could stay here for the weekend..." he breathed as he began kissing me on my neck...

"We could..." I breathed...

"We could leave on Monday..." he breathed in my ear as he led me into the master bedroom...

"We could..." I breathed as he pushed his tongue in my mouth...

"And we could go back to your place...

"Mmm Hmmm..."

"And get married on Tuesday..." he breathed as he pushed me down on my back...

"Darnell... wait..." Darnell ignored me and lay down on top of me...

"Why..." he growled in my ear...

"Because... I need to go shopping..."

"You need to go shopping? Now?"

"Yes..."

"I'll take you shopping..." he breathed as he ran his hand down my body to my waist... "As soon as we're done..."

"You can't take me..."

"Why can't I take you?" he breathed as he moved his right hand up to my breast and squeezed...

"I can't let you see my dress..." I moaned before he pushed his tongue in my mouth...

"Mmmm... Let me make love to you... and you'll have the rest of the day to go shopping..." he breathed as he moved his hand down to my waist and opened my pants...

"Welcome to Dresses By Hilda – I'm Hilda..." she greeted as she extended her hand...

"I'm Chelle..."

"How can I make your day unforgettable?" She asked...

"I saw this pantsuit online..."

"Do you have a picture?"

"Yes..." I answered as I gave her my cell phone...

"Oh my goodness... This dress is stunning... and so are you..."

"Thank you..."

"Today is your lucky day – I just got that dress in about an hour ago..."

"Oh my God!" I exclaimed...

"C'mon – let's get you into the dressing room..." she said as she took me by the hand and led me into the dressing room.... "Have you ever been here before?"

"No..."

"What brought you to my shop?"

"My fiancé lives here so I googled bridal shops in the area and I read the reviews..."

"Thank you – I'll go get your pantsuit – you get undressed..."

"Okay..." When she came into the dressing room, I was startled...

"I'm sorry – would you prefer some privacy?"

"No – I need your help..."

"Okay – I'll help you step into your pantsuit..." she said as she guided me into it. I got the pantsuit on and she led me out the dressing room to the full-length mirror... and I cried... "You don't like it?"

"This... This is the one..."

"I agree..." she sighed. I chose a sequined casual baguette two-piece jumpsuit what was anything but casual. The jumpsuit featured a half high neck connected with details that went along the neck down to my feet. The attached white cloak coat made me look more elegant than I already did...

"I'm going to need his help getting dressed..." I sighed...

"You can't let him help you get dressed..."

"It's just the two of us..."

"Where are you getting married?"

"We're getting married in White Plains in City Hall…"

"You must be in a hurry – how long have you been engaged?"

"We just got engaged today…" I sighed…

"I can't believe how great you look in that dress – do you have shoes?"

"I have shoes…"

"I have some shoes that would go great with your pantsuit if you'd like to try them on…"

"Sure…" I sighed. I continued to admire myself in the mirror as she went to get the shoes. When she came back, I started to sit down but she stopped me…

"Uh Uh – let me help you…" she commanded as she lifted my foot, took off my shoe, put on the shoe she wanted me to try on, and turned me towards the mirror…

"These are pretty!" I exclaimed…

"Here – let's put the other one on…" she said as she picked up my other foot, took off my shoe, and put on the other shoe…"

"I want them!" I exclaimed…

"Good – I'll get this bagged for you – Can I ask you something?"

"Sure…"

"Do you really want to get married in City Hall?"

"Well… Since I want to get married right away…"

"I have a friend at the Metropolis Country Club in White Plains – let me give them a call..." she said as she went to go make the call. I continued to admire myself in the full-length mirror...

"Hello Hilda..." Kathy answered...

"Hello Kathy – I need your help...

"What can I do for you?"

"There's a beautiful young lady that just bought the sequined casual baguette two-piece jumpsuit I ordered – and she's getting married in City Hall in White Plains on Tuesday..."

"Oh no – we can't let that happened – let me see if we have a cancelation – hold on..." she said as she put Hilda on hold... "Hilda – we have 10 a.m. available if she's interested..."

"She's interested!" Hilda exclaimed...

"Are you sure?"

"I'm sure – I'll make sure – she'll see you on Tuesday morning!"

"Hilda – wait!"

"Yes Kathy?"

"How many people are in their party?"

"It's just the two of them..."

"Oh that's good – we can give them a nice wedding and a nice breakfast..."

"Thank you Kathy..." Hilda sighed...

"You're welcome – make sure the bride is here at 9:00 – we want her to be ready before 10..."

"I sure will – I'll tell her now – thank you again!"

"You're welcome – what's her name?"

"I don't know!" she laughed...

"That's okay – I'll just put Hilda in the book for 10..."

"Thank you so much – I owe you..."

"Nonsense – it's the least I can do for you with all the referrals you've given us over the years..."

"Okay – I'll go tell her now!" she exclaimed as she hung up and hurried back over to me... "You're all set – I'm going to bag up your pantsuit and shoes – but you're not getting married in City Hall on Tuesday..."

"I'm not? Why?"

"I'm sorry honey – I couldn't let you do that – not in this pantsuit – you're going to be getting married at the Metropolis Country Club at 10 – make sure you're there at 9 – never mind – I'll write everything down for you..." she said as she grabbed one of her cards and wrote down the information... "Her name is Kathy Trepp – her number is on the card – when you get there tell her Hilda sent you – she'll take care of you..."

"Thank you..." I sighed as I started crying...

"The only crying allowed in here is happy tears – so those are happy tears – right?"

"Yea..." I sniffed...

"Good – now give me a hug!" she exclaimed as she pulled me into a hug and held me as if I was her daughter... "Okay - I'm going to bag this up for real this time..." she laughed as she helped me out of the pantsuit. I lifted my feet one at a time, let her help me out of the shoes, and went back into the dressing room...

"City Clerk's office – this is Ms. Hurley..."

"Amy – this is Kathy from Metropolis..."

"Hello Kathy – how are you?"

"Do you have a wedding scheduled on Tuesday morning?"

"Yes – how'd you know?"

"It's been moved to the Metropolis at 10..."

"I thought they were getting married here?"

"You know how Hilda is..." Kathy laughed...

"Oh I know exactly how Hilda is – nobody gets married in City Hall wearing a dress by Hilda!" Amy laughed...

"Can you officiate the wedding here at 10?"

"I'll be there – I'll just let them know I'm officiating a wedding at the Metropolis – who could say no to that?"

"Thank you Amy – I appreciate it..."

"You're welcome..."

"Amy?"

"Yes Kathy?"

"What are their names?"

"Chelle & Darnell Tompkins..."

"Got it – thanks!" Kathy exclaimed as she hung up...

"I might as well go out while she's out..." Darnell said as he got up. Darnell didn't even bother looking online for tuxedo shops in the area... "I'm going right over to David's Bridal..." he said as he locked the door...

"Welcome to David's Bridal – My name is Jessica – how may I help you?"

"I'm Darnell – I'm looking for a classic tux..." he answered...

"Is it for you?"

"Yea..." he sighed...

"When's the big day?"

"We're getting married on Tuesday..."

"Tuesday?! Oh my goodness – I hope we have something for you on such short notice..." she said as she hurried over to the tuxedos and Darnell followed... "What size are you?"

"Jacket size 40 regular – pants 38 by 32..."

"Uh Huh..." she said as she looked through the tuxedos... "How 'bout this one?" she asked as she held up the Shawl Collar Tuxedo made of 100% super-fine Italian Merino Wool. The jacket had a one-button closure and a100% silk satin shawl collar. The pants were fully canvassed.

"I like it..." he sighed...

"It's one of our best sellers..."

"I can see why..."

"Here – go try it on..." she said as she handed it to him. Darnell went into the dressing room and tried on the suit. He admired himself in the mirror for a few moments and then Jessica called him... "How's it going Darnell?"

"You tell me..." he answered as he came out the dressing room...

"If you were my fiancé and I saw you wearing that at the altar – I'd jump your bones!"

"Thanks..." Darnell said as he smiled...

"It looks really good on you..." she sighed...

"I'll take it..."

"I thought you would – would you like a dress shirt? We have a wing Collar Fly Front Dress Shirt that looks great with that tux..."

'I'll take that too..."

"What size?"

"18 – Sleeve 20 inches..."

"We have that..." she said as she picked one up... "Would you like a bowtie or a regular tie?"

"I'll take a regular tie..."

"Silk or satin?"

"Satin..."

"The only thing you need now is shoes!" she exclaimed as Darnell followed her over to the men's shoes...

"I'll take those right there in a size 9..." he said as he pointed to the Black Patent Leather Shoes...

"Those are nice... and they're comfortable..."

"Thank you..."

"You're all set – I'll get you out of here in a few minutes..." she said as she walked to the front of the store and Darnell followed her...

"Thanks again..." he said...

"You're welcome Darnell" she said as Darnell left...

"I bet I'll beat Chelle home..." he laughed to himself as he got in the Uber. He laughed again as his Uber and my Uber pulled up at the same time...

"Hey..." I sighed...

"Hey..." The Ubers drove off and we stood there for a moment... "I guess we should go inside now..." he said as he went to open the door and I followed...

"I'll be right back..." I said as I went into the master bedroom and opened the closet. I regretted it as soon as I opened it...

"Hey Chelle – I..." Darnell stopped talking mid-sentence...

"I see you haven't had a chance to clean out the closets..."

"I'm sorry – I didn't have a chance – that's not true – I forgot – I know I should've..."

"Is this her wedding dress?" I interrupted...

"Yea..."

"It's really pretty – I think I'll donate it..."

"Donate it?"

"Yea – consignment shops take donations all the time – this dress will make someone a beautiful bride one day..."

"I guess..."

"She always did know how to dress – I'll donate all her things – it'd be a shame to dispose of her clothes..." I said as I went through her clothes... "I'll get rid of this one..." I said as I picked up a rust-colored pantsuit trimmed in black...

"That was one of her favorite outfits!" he laughed...

"I'm going to do the world a favor..." I said as I took it off the hanger and put it in the basket...

"You shouldn't have to do that – let me..."

"Darnell – stop..."

"Okay..."

"It is what it is – this was her house – it's not unusual to see her things in here..."

"The last thing I wanted was for you to go shopping for your wedding dress only to come back here and see her wedding dress..." he sighed...

"C'mon – let's go in the guest room – unless she has clothes in there too..."

"She does..."

"What about the other room with the beds in it?" Darnell didn't answer me – he just shook his head...

"Oh well – I guess I can put my things in the coat closet in the hallway..." I said as I started to walk out the bedroom...

"Chelle – wait..."

"Oh c'mon!" I laughed...

"I'll move her things into the guest room and then you can put your things in here..."

"I'll help you..." I said as I put my bags on the bed, went into the closet, and grabbed a bunch of clothes out the closet. Darnell stood there for a few moments as I left to put her things in the guest room but when I came back, he had a bunch of clothes in his hands too... "This won't take long..." I said as I grabbed another bunch of clothes. We both continued to go back and forth until we had all of her clothes out the closet...

"What are you going to do with her shoes?"

"Most of them are barely worn – I'll donate them to the consignment shop – those shoes over there are going in the garbage!" I laughed. Darnell just smiled at me and we continued to empty her things out the closet. "What's in this drawer?" I asked as I went to open it...

"That's her jewelry..."

"Oh okay – I can donate that to the consignment shop too..."

"I figured you'd want to pawn it..." he laughed...

"You don't pawn fine jewelry – that's disrespectful..." I said as I took the drawer out and brought it into the guest room. I went into the walk-in closet, found an empty drawer and put the jewelry in it. I saw Darnell's wedding band and I picked it up to read the inscription... 'Darnell & Dana – Now & Forever.' As soon as I read the inscription, I started crying...

"Chelle? You okay in there?"

"No..." Darnell came running into the guest room and saw me looking at the inscription on his wedding band...

"Chelle... Don't cry... Please..." he whispered as he teared up...

"I'm okay..." I sniffed... "It's just that when you gave me the bracelet..."

"I know..." he whispered as he held me...

"Did we get everything out the closet?"

"The only thing left in there is the wedding dress..."

"I'll get the wedding dress – you go get the coats out the coat closet and I'll help you after I get the wedding dress..."

"Okay..." Darnell really didn't want to let me go but he did and I went to get her wedding dress out the closet...

"This is beautiful... but not for me..." I said as I took it into the guest room and hung it up. Darnell was coming in with coats from the coat closet as I came out... "Did you get everything?"

"There's a few coats left in there..."

"I'll get them..." I said as I left the room. I went to the hall closet, grabbed the remaining coats, and took them back to the guest room...

"I'll get her boots..." Darnell said as he left the room to go get them and I followed... "You don't have to help me – I got it..." I deliberately ignored him, went in the closet, picked up a few pairs of boots, took them into the guest room, and put them in the closet...

"Darnell? Darnell – you in there?"

"Who's that?" I asked...

"That's Dana's friend – Helen..." he answered as he went to open the door...

"Hey Darnell – I was wondering when I was gonna run into you again..."

"Hello Helen..."

"You mind if I come in?"

"Now's not a good time..."

"I understand – you still grieving and all..." she said as she pulled him into a hug...

"Thanks for that..." he said as he pulled away...

"I'm here for you if you need anything..." she whispered in his ear before she walked away...

"Ewww!" he exclaimed as he shut the door and I bust out laughing...

"I'm here for you if you need anything..." I teased...

"That woman has been trying to push up on me ever since I buried Dana..." he laughed...

"That'll stop as soon as I introduce myself..." I laughed...

"Damn right it will..." he laughed...

"C'mon – let's go put our things in our closet..." I said as I took his hand and led him into the master bedroom. We picked up our things, put them in the closet, and Darnell kissed me... "We need to talk..."

"Okay..." he sighed as he followed me into the living room and we both sat down...

"I thought she was my now and forever..."

"I know – but that's not what we need to talk about..."

"What do we need to talk about then?"

"We need to talk about the wedding..."

"You still wanna get married – right?"

"Of course I do!"

"Okay – just checking..."

"I went to Dresses By Hilda today..."

"Oohh..."

"What does that mean?"

"Nothing – go ahead..."

"Dana went there too – didn't she?"

"Yea..."

"Okay – so anyway – Hilda said she couldn't let me get married in City Hall so she called Kathy at Metropolis..."

"The country club in White Plains?"

"Yes..."

"Are you telling me..."

"We're getting married in the Clubhouse at Metropolis on Tuesday at 10..." I interrupted...

"We need to call Ms. Hurley and tell her we've made other arrangements..."

"Kathy already took care of that..."

"I love you..."

"I love you too – but I need to talk to you about something else..."

"Okay..."

"We need to go to Raymour & Flannigan..."

"I knew it..." he laughed...

"You knew I wouldn't like this furniture?"

"Yea..." he laughed...

"How'd you know I wouldn't like it?"

"I knew you wouldn't like it..." he laughed... "Because I don't like it!" We both bust out laughing...

"Ahh Haa Haa Haa Haa Haa!"

"Darnell..."

"Huh?"

"It's 7 o'clock..."

"I'm tired..."

"So am I – but they'll be here at 9..."

"Okay..." he sighed as he got up and went into the kitchen to make coffee...

After we moved all of Dana's things into the guest room, I called Cosign It On Main. I explained that we had a lot of things to donate to their shop, including furniture, and they were very happy. I spoke with Dom first and she explained the process. After speaking with her, I spoke with Candice to give her our information and arrange a pick-up. We spent Friday night and all day Saturday moving things from the walk-in closet in the office to the guest room and I was just as tired as Darnell. Thank God Mondays are appointment-only because we needed a few hours to get all her items out of there...

"Chelle?"

"Yes Darnell?"

"Coffee's ready." I went into the kitchen and sat at the island as he put a cup of coffee in front of me...

"Oh my God – thank you!" I sighed as I sipped...

"You're welcome..." he said as he sat down with me...

"Are you sure you're okay with me giving them all the furniture?"

"I'm okay with whatever you want to do..."

"I love you..."

"I love you too..."

"Will you come shopping with me?"

"Do I have to?"

"Well... you don't have to... but I'd like your input..."

"You would?"

"Why wouldn't I? I want you to be comfortable in our home..."

"You said our home..." he sighed as he smiled...

"Stop that!"

"What am I doing?"

"You're making me want to go back to bed!"

"What's wrong with that?"

"If I go back to bed – I won't want to get up..."

"Like I said – what's wrong with that?"

"We need to get ready..."

"I'm not happy right now..."

"I'll make it up to you..." I said as I finished my coffee and got up. I thought I was going to take a shower by myself but Darnell had other ideas...

"Hello..." he whispered in my ear as he came up behind me and pulled me close to him...

"Hello..." I giggled. Darnell turned me around, pulled me into a kiss, and we spent the next 45 minutes competing in the Sexual Olympics... "Darnell..." I panted...

"Don't make me stop..."

"My phone is ringing..."

"Okay..." he sighed as he let me down. I hurried to answer my phone...

"Good morning..."

"Good morning Chelle – this is Dom from Cosign – are we still on for today?"

"Yes..." I answered as Darnell came up behind me and began kissing me on my neck...

"Okay – we're going to bring a van and a U-Haul – we're moving the furniture separately..."

"Okay..."

"You have a lot of things so the process is going to take a few hours – is that okay?"

"That's fine..."

"And you're sure about donating everything to the shop?"

"I'm sure..."

"Okay – we'll itemize everything and give you a receipt for tax purposes..."

"Okay..."

"Alright then – we'll see you in about 30 minutes..." she said as she hung up...

"That doesn't give us much time..." Darnell breathed in my ear...

"No it doesn't – we need to get dressed!" I laughed as I pulled away from him...

"Good morning..." Helen greeted as she came outside...

"Good morning..." Dom greeted. Helen watched as the U-Haul pulled up behind the van...

"Y'all movers?" she asked...

"No – we're from Cosign..." Dom answered...

"Cosign? What's that? They gettin' a loan or y'all have to repo?"

"No Maam – we're from a consignment shop in the area. His wife's things are being donated to our shop..."

"Donated?! Y'all not buying that stuff?!"

"It was nice meeting you – we need to go get started..." Dom answered as Candice followed her to our door...

"Good morning..." I greeted...

"Good morning..." Dom laughed... "I'm Dom, this is Candice, and that's your nosey neighbor!" she laughed...

"She probably thinks we're moving..." Darnell said as he came out into the living room...

"Naa – we told her we're from Cosign and she thought we were here to repo your stuff!" Candice laughed...

"Oh my God!" Darnell exclaimed as we all laughed...

"I tried to explain that you were donating his wife's things and she frowned up her face and said donated – y'all not buying that stuff?" Dom laughed...

"Well damn – I wasn't aware we needed her permission!" Darnell laughed...

"Okay – where would you like to start?"

"We can start in the guest room..." I said as I went towards the guest room and they both followed...

"Wow! You have an entire store in here!" Dom exclaimed...

"They sure do!" Candice agreed...

"Let's start with the jewelry..." I suggested...

"Okay..." Dom agreed. I went to get the jewelry and they followed me into the kitchen...

"Wow... These are some beautiful pieces..." Candice sighed. Dom began writing a list and tagged each piece as Candice continued to admire the jewelry...

"We can't take this one..." Candice said as she handed me Darnell's wedding band...

"Is that because they're engraved?" Darnell asked...

"Yes..." Dom answered as she continued writing and tagging... "Okay – I'm done with the jewelry – are you sure you don't want anything before I take this?"

"I don't want anything..."

"Okay – I'll be right back..." she said as she got up to go outside...

"Whatchu got there?" Helen asked...

"This is her jewelry..."

"Oh!! Can I see?!"

"I'm sorry – once it's been tagged – I can't..." Dom answered as she opened the van, put the box inside, closed the door, locked it, and came back inside laughing...

"What's so funny?" Candice asked...

"Your neighbor is something else..." Dom answered as she shook her head...

"I'll be right back..." I said as I went got up and went into the bedroom. I took the outfit out the basket, put it on a hanger, and brought it into the living room...

"What are you doing with that?" Darnell asked...

"I'm going to offer it to Helen..." I answered...

"Wait – let's write and tag a few outfits and then you can offer Helen the outfit..." Candice suggested...

"That's a good idea..." Dom said as she got up and we went into the guest room. Darnell started breakfast while we were tagging and my stomach started growling...

"Me too!" Dom exclaimed as we all laughed...

"Ladies – breakfast will be ready in a few minutes – can you take a break?"

"Sure – I just want us to get these clothes out to the van first..." Dom answered...

"Let me help you with that..." Darnell said as he turned the flame down and went to take some clothes from Dom...

When we got outside, Helen was watching us so I took it upon myself to go over and offer her the outfit...

"Helen – they can't take this outfit – would you like it?"

"Who the hell are you and what the hell are you doing with Dana's things?!"

"That's my fiancée..." Darnell answered as he walked up on our conversation...

"Your fiancée?!"

"Yes – and I'd appreciate it if you showed her some respect..."

"Show respect to her for what?! Your wife hasn't even been dead a week and you already have a new Bitch talkin' 'bout she's your fiancée – you don't have any fuckin' respect – I see why she cheated on your ass!!"

"What the fuck did you just say?!" Darnell gritted as he raised his hand to slap her and I stepped between them...

"You gon' hit me?! You gon' hit me over this Bitch?!"

"SLAP!!" I slapped her so quick I shocked myself...

"Oh no you didn't!! Bitch I'll fuck you up!!" she gritted as she lunged towards me and Darnell grabbed her...

"Take your muthafuckin' hands off me!!" Darnell ignored her as he carried her over to her entryway and put her down...

"Do yourself a favor – stay out of our way!!" We looked on in shock as Helen stormed into her house and slammed the door... "I'm very sorry ladies..." he sighed as he came back over to take the rest of the clothes from Candice...

"It's fine – let's get these in the van – I hope the food didn't burn 'cause I'm hungry!" Dom exclaimed as we finished putting the clothes in the van and went inside. Darnell rushed over to the stove and checked on the food...

"We're good!" he exclaimed as he took down four plates...

"That was delicious – thank you!" Dom exclaimed...

"Yes – thank you!" Candice exclaimed as there was a knock on the door...

"Who is it?" Darnell asked...

"Police..." Darnell went to open the door...

"Hello Officer Nunn..."

"Do I know you?"

"Can we talk outside?"

"Sure..."

"We might as well write and tag some more clothes..." I suggested as Darnell went outside and closed the door...

"You met me at the airport..."

"The airport?"

"You were one of the officers that told me my wife died..."

"Oh that's right – sorry for you loss..."

"Thank you..."

"I'm sorry to be here while you're grieving but your neighbor called us – she says she was assaulted by your – I won't say..."

"I'm sorry. My neighbor was good friends with my wife. My fiancée has been helping me go through her things and Helen became belligerent and threatened her so my fiancée defended herself..."

"So your neighbor threated your fiancée and your fiancée slapped her in self-defense?"

"Yes..." he answered as we came outside...

"That's her!" Helen yelled...

"May I speak with you a moment?" Officer Nunn asked...

"Sure – let help them get these in the van." Officer Nunn waited for me and I went to speak with him...

"What's your name?"

"Chelle Robinson..."

"You're his fiancée?"

"Yes..."

"Your neighbor called to press charges against you because you slapped her..."

"That's true..."

"Your fiancé told us she was belligerent towards you and she threatened you so you slapped her in self-defense – is that what happened?"

"That's exactly what happened officer – she even offered her an outfit..." Dom answered as she came over...

"Who are you Maam?"

"I'm Dom from Cosign..."

"Downtown?"

"Yes..."

"Nice to meet you – my wife loves to shop in your store..."

"I'm happy to hear that..."

"I have what I need – I'll let you get back to what you were doing..." he said as he went to talk to Helen...

"That's bullshit! I should be able to press charges!"

"I'm sorry Maam – but they're all saying you were being belligerent, you threatened her, and she slapped you in self-defense..."

"Fuck you!" she exclaimed as she slammed her door. Officer Nunn shook his head and laughed to himself as he went to get back in his car and we all went back inside to continue tagging...

We went to take a nap on the only thing left in the house – the master bed. Everything else was gone...

"Darnell..." I yawned...

"Yes Chelle?" he answered as he yawned and stretched...

"I need to tell you something..." I said as I sat up...

"Okay..."

"I used the bathroom earlier..."

"You don't need to tell me that – I heard you!" he laughed...

"Darnell..."

"Yes Chelle?"

"I looked in the medicine cabinet..."

"Oh..."

"It's gone..."

"It's gone?"

"I flushed them down the toilet..."

"You did? Why?"

"Because you don't need them anymore..." I answered as I pulled him into a kiss...

"I love you..."

"I love you too..."

"Are you hungry?"

"Starving..."

"I'll order some Chinese food..." he said as he picked up his phone...

"Chelle..." Darnell whispered as he kissed me awake...

"Yes Darnell..." I sighed with my eyes closed...

'We're getting married today..." he breathed as he kissed me again...

"Mmm... I know..." I breathed as I kissed him back...

"I can't believe I'm going to be making love to my wife in a few hours...."

"I'm going to be making love to my husband...

"Let's get in the shower..."

"Okay – but we have to get in and get out..."

"Why?"

"Because I don't want to be late for our wedding..."

"We can be quick..." he breathed as he kissed my neck..."

"I don't wanna be quick..."

"Are you sure?" he breathed in my ear as he grabbed my breast and squeezed it...

"I'm sure... Let's get up..."

"I'm already up..." he breathed as he took my hand and rubbed his dick with it...

"I'm sorry Darnell – I need you to wait until after we're married..." I sighed as I sat up..."

"I can't believe you just said that to me!" he laughed...

"C'mon – let's go get in the shower..." I laughed as I got up out the bed...

"You want coffee?"

"No – I want my first cup of coffee to be with my husband..."

"I love you..."

"I love you too..." I sighed as I headed toward the bathroom and he followed...

"Are you ready to become Mrs. Tompkins?"

"I'm ready..."

"Okay – Let's do this!" he exclaimed as we went downstairs...

"Good morning Ms. Robinson..." Robert greeted as he opened the door to the limo...

"Good morning Robert – is this for us?"

"Yes Maam..."

"Good morning Robert – Thank you..." Darnell said...

"You're welcome Sir..." Robert said as we got in and headed towards the Metropolis...

"It sure is beautiful here..." I sighed...

"Wait 'till you see the inside..." Darnell said as he helped me out of the limo and we went inside...

"Good morning – you must be Chelle – I'm Kathy – come with me – Darnell – you go with him..." she commanded as she took my hand and a man went towards Darnell...

"This way please..." he requested...

"Umm... our things are in the limo..." Darnell said...

"I'm Ken – we'll make sure you get your things – please come with me..."

"Okay..." Darnell agreed as they went off in the opposite direction...

"Come with me Chelle..." Kathy commanded as she led me to the ladies room...

"Wow – this is nice..." I sighed...

"I'm going to help you touch up your hair and make-up, and then I'll help you get dressed – I'll be right back..."

"Thanks for showing me where the men's room is – I think I can take in from here..." Darnell laughed...

"I didn't bring you here to go to the bathroom – I brought you here so you can get dressed and then I'm going to make sure you get to the Clubhouse without your bride seeing you – I'll be right back – feel free to use the bathroom if you need to..." Ken said as he hurried out the bathroom...

"Gee thanks..." Darnell laughed as he went to pee...

"I think we got everything..." Kathy breathed...

"I think so too – let's go get these two married!" Ken exclaimed as they hurried back inside...

"You're going to make a beautiful bride..." Kathy sighed as she finished touching up my make-up..."

"Thank you – I usually do my own make-up..."

"You deserve something extra on your wedding day..." she said as she moved my head to the side, putting the finishing touches on my hair... "Okay – let's get you out of those clothes and into your wedding dress..."

"I'm not wearing a wedding dress..."

"You're not?! Why?!"

"You'll see..." I answered as she pulled out the pantsuit and jacket...

"Oh my God! This is gorgeous!"

"Thank you..."

"Hurry up – I need to see you in this!" I got undressed as she gestured for me to come over to her. I started to cry as she helped me into my pantsuit...

"Oh no – Don't do that!' she exclaimed as she grabbed a few tissues and dabbed my eyes...

"I can't help it..."

"You need to try – we can't have your make-up running when we take pictures!" she exclaimed as she turned me around...

"Give me your foot..." I gave her my left foot, she put my shoe on, and then I gave her my right foot... "Okay – now let me look at you..." she sighed as she stood up... "You're ready – wait here!" she exclaimed as she rushed out the bathroom...

"You started without me..." Ken laughed as he came back into the bathroom...

"I've been dressing and undressing myself for a long time..." Darnell laughed...

"I'm sure you have – I just want to make sure you put your best foot forward for your bride...

"Fuck you talkin' 'bout – I got two great feet!" he exclaimed as he started doing the two-step...

"Okay! I see you!" Ken exclaimed as he got up... "I got a little something in me too!" he exclaimed as he started dancing...

"Okay, okay – how 'bout you dance on over there and get my suit for me before someone comes in here and wonders why I'm dancing in my boxers with you..." Darnell laughed as he sat on the bench...

"Okay!" Ken exclaimed as he took the suit out the bag along with the shirt, tie, socks, and shoes. He handed the socks to Darnell, waited for Darnell to put them on, and then he handed Darnell the pants... "Nice..." Ken sighed...

"I'll take the shoes..." Darnell said. Ken handed him the shoes, he put them on, stood up, and admired himself in the mirror...

"Looking good!" Ken exclaimed as he handed Darnell the shirt. Darnell put the shirt on, Ken handed him the tie, and Darnell checked himself in the mirror again. Ken handed him the jacket and when Darnell put it on, he got excited... "Damn! She's going to jump your bones! C'mon!" he exclaimed as he hurried to open the door and gestured for Darnell to follow him out the men's room, down the hall, and into the Clubhouse...

"You look good Darnell – I'll go get your bride now..." Kathy said as she hurried out the Clubhouse...

"Are they ready?" Amy asked as she came in with her assistant, Alice...

"Yes – they're ready... Kathy answered as she hurried to come get me...

"Chelle – it's time!" she exclaimed as she opened the bathroom door... "Don't you dare!" she laughed as I dabbed my eyes with tissues and held them in my hand as she led me to the Clubhouse...

"Chelle..." Darnell whispered as he started crying. I hurried over to him and dabbed his eyes with the tissues I was holding...

"I give up!" Kathy laughed as Ken took pictures. I was so happy that this moment was being captured...

"It's time..." Amy said. I put the tissues in Darnell's pocket and Amy began...

"Kathy – do you have Chelle's cell phone?"

"Yes..." she answered...

"Please give it to Alice..." Kathy gave my phone to Alice as she was instructed...

"Okay – I need you both to stand here and face each other..." Amy commanded...

"Okay..." we both said as we stood facing each other and took hands...

"Start recording Alice..."

"Okay..." Alice said...

"Beloved... we are gathered here this morning to join Chelle Robinson and Darnell Tompkins in marriage. You have both come before me, expressed your desire to become husband and wife, and you're both in a hurry!"

she said as she laughed along with us. "Do you have rings?"

"Yes – we have rings..." Darnell answered as he took two ring boxes out his pocket...

"Okay – take the rings out the boxes – Chelle – you take his ring – Darnell – you take her ring..."

"Okay..." we both said as I took his ring and he took mine...

"Okay – Darnell – do you have anything you want to say to Chelle?"

"Yes I do..." Darnell answered as he took my hands... "Chelle – I had no idea that God was working when my Uber got cancelled and I ended up going to the airport with you. I've only known you for a 26 days and I fell in love with you in 5 days. Today, you're making me the happiest man in the world. Thank you for loving me back..." I didn't wait for Amy to ask as I responded to Darnell...

"Darnell – I had no idea that God was working when you ended up in my Uber, but I know exactly how I feel. From the moment you touched my hand and I felt your breath I've wanted you. You make me feel loved and wanted in ways I've always dreamed about and I'm so happy God brought us together to make that happen. Today – you're making me the happiest I've ever been in my life – and I know it's only going to get better from here. Thank you for choosing me..."

117

"I love you so much..." Darnell breathed as he kissed me...

"We're not finished..." Amy laughed...

"Sorry – I couldn't help it..." Darnell laughed...

"That's alright – Darnell, I took it upon myself to choose your vows – repeat after me..."

"Okay – I'm ready..."

"Chelle – I take you as my wife, with your faults and your strengths, as I offer myself to you with my faults and my strengths..." Darnell repeated after Amy and then she continued... "I will help you when you need help and turn to you when I need help. Today - I choose to spend the rest of my life with you..." I started crying as Darnell repeated the vows to me and he took the tissues out of his pocket, dabbed my eyes, and put them back in his pocket. When he was finished, I took his face in my hands and kissed him. Amy shook her head and laughed... "Okay Chelle – repeat after me..."

"Okay – I'm ready..."

"Darnell..." I said... and then I started crying. Darnell took the tissues out his pocket, dabbed my eyes again, put them back in his pocket, and then I continued...

"I take you as my as my husband, with your faults and your strengths, as I offer myself to you with my faults and my strengths. I will help you when you need help and turn to you when I need help. Today – I choose to spend the rest of my life with you..." Darnell started crying as I repeated the vows to him and he took the tissues out of his pocket again, dabbed his eyes again, and put them back in his pocket. When he was finished, I took his face in my hands and kissed him...

"By the power invested in me by the State of New York and the City of White Plains – I now pronounce you husband and wife. Darnell – you may kiss your bride – again!" A few people started to gather outside and everyone erupted in applause as Darnell and I held each other and kissed. "Everyone – I present to you – Mr. and Mrs. Darnell Tompkins!" Amy exclaimed as the applause continued. Alice stopped recording and started taking pictures as Darnell and I hugged Amy and she hugged us back... and then she started crying...

"Aww..." Everyone said as Alice captured it in the pictures...

"How soon will we get our marriage certificate?" Darnell asked...

"You'll get it in about a week or so..."

"Can you send it to my address?" I asked...

"I'll make sure Vital Records sends it there..."

"Thank you Ms. Hurley..." I said...

"Please – call me Amy..."

"Thank you Amy..." I sighed...

"Yes Amy – thank you..." Darnell sighed...

"You're welcome – now go get your phone from Alice – congratulations..." she said as she hugged us both, Alice gave Darnell my phone, and they both left...

"We have a gift for you..." Kathy said as Ken continued taking pictures...

"You do?" We both asked...

"Kathy didn't answer us. She opened the door to the Clubhouse and we watched as the chef rolled in a table filled with a complete breakfast...

"Thank you so much..." I cried. Darnell took the tissues out his pocket and dabbed my eyes along with his...

"You're welcome – we don't have anyone else scheduled for the Clubhouse until 2 p.m. so relax, enjoy your breakfast, and make sure you go outside and take in the grounds...

"We will – thank you!" Darnell exclaimed as Ken continued to take pictures...

"I'm going to capture every moment until you leave – if that's alright..." Ken said...

"That's fine!" I exclaimed as we sat down to eat...

"Would you like some coffee Mrs. Tompkins?" Darnell asked...

"Yes Mr. Tompkins..." I sighed. Darnell made us both a cup of coffee with hazelnut creamer, stirred it, and placed a cup in front of me...

"Here's to our first cup of coffee as husband and wife..."

"Here's to our first cup of coffee as husband and wife..." I repeated as we both took a sip. We continued to sit in the Clubhouse as we enjoyed scrambled eggs with white cheddar, turkey sausage, turkey bacon, potatoes with onions, red peppers, green peppers, assorted fruits, toasted croissants with butter, and waffles with maple syrup...

"Good afternoon Ms. Robinson – welcome back..." Robert greeted...

"Mrs. Tompkins..." Darnell corrected...

"You're married?!" Robert exclaimed...

"Yes..." Darnell sighed...

"Congratulations..."

"Thank you..." we both said as Darnell took my hand and rushed me towards the elevator. When we got upstairs, Darnell couldn't wait to take me up on what I promised him earlier...

"Come here Mrs. Tompkins..." he commanded...

"No..."

"Umm... Wait... What?"

"I said no..."

"I'm not waiting another minute..."

"It'll be worth it... I promise..."

"Okay... I'll wait..." he said as he sat down on the couch...

"Where are the tissues we used when we were crying?"

"They're still in my pocket – why?"

"I need to put them in a bag..."

"Umm... okay... here..." he said as he took them out his pocket and handed them to me. Darnell watched me put them in a zip lock bag...

"I'm going to frame them in a 3D frame and name it 'Tears of Joy'..."

"I love you..." he whispered as he started crying. I hurried over to him and dabbed his eyes with the tissues again and put them back in the bag...

"Okay – hurry up – I'm waiting..."

"Yes Mr. Tompkins..." I said as I hurried into the bedroom. As soon as I got in the bedroom, I took off my clothes and put on a white silk bikini that left nothing to the imagination. The bikini was hugging me in all the right places with my breasts completely exposed as well as my pussy. I checked myself out in front of the mirror in the bathroom before I went over to the window, got on the floor on my knees, spread my legs open, and put my arms at my sides...

"Mr. Tompkins?"

"Yes Mrs. Tompkins?"

"'You can come get me now..." Darnell smiled to himself as he got up and took his time coming into the bedroom...

"Damn..."

"You like?" I asked...

"I love..." he breathed as he came over to me, stood in front of me, and put his hands on his hips...

"What can I do for you?" Darnell stepped away from me, kicked off his shoes, and came back over in front of me...

"Take my pants off..." he commanded. I unbuckled his belt, unbuttoned his pants, took down the zipper, and pulled his pants down along with his boxers. Darnell stepped out of his pants and boxers, and spread his legs as his dick sprang to attention. I waited for him to tell me what he wanted me to do next as he began tapping the head of his dick on my lips... "Open your mouth..." I did as was told. Darnell put both of his hands on the sides of my head, and began to slowly push his dick in my mouth as the sun was shining through the window...

"Good morning Mrs. Tompkins...

"Good morning Mr. Tompkins..."

"Are you sure you wanna do this?"

"I'm sure..."

"Okay – I'm going to get in the shower..." he sighed as he got up...

"I'll be in there in a minute..." I sighed as I got up. Darnell started the shower and I knew I didn't have long... "Where is it?!" I exclaimed as I looked all over the bedroom... "There you are!" I exclaimed as I found my phone and began looking through the pictures... "I'll send her this one..." I said as I forwarded the picture to Veronica with the following message... "Mr. & Mrs. Tompkins, Tuesday, January 17th, 2023...."

"Chelle?"

"Coming!" I answered as I hurried into the bathroom...

"What the fuck?! Veronica exclaimed as she opened the message... "Oh shit!!"

"Who are you calling?" Darnell asked me as he made coffee...

"I'm calling Veronica..." I answered as I dialed her number...

"Good morning – I guess you won't be coming into work today..."

"I'll be in – I'm calling because I need you to let Steph know that I'm going to personnel before I come in..."

"Okay – I'll see you later..." she said as she hung up. I was hurt because she didn't congratulate me and Darnell noticed it...

"What's wrong?"

"Nothing..." I sighed...

"What's wrong?"

"She didn't congratulate me..."

"Give her time – she'll come around..." he said as he pulled me into a kiss...

"I love you..."

"I love you too – drink your coffee so we can get to personnel..."

"Okay..." I sighed. Darnell smiled at me and I started drinking my coffee before he could say anything else...

"Good morning Darnell..." Kevin greeted. Kevin took my hand and we kept walking towards Victoria's office...

"Good morning – what brings you both here so early?" she asked...

"We need to update our paperwork..." I answered...

"We?" she asked...

"We got married yesterday..." Darnell added...

"Oh my God – get up!" she exclaimed. We both got up and she hurried from behind her desk... "Congratulations!" she exclaimed as she pulled us both into a hug...

"What's all the excitement about?" Kevin asked as he stuck his head in the door...

"They got married!" Victoria blurted out...

"Congratulations..." Kevin said. Darnell got up and closed the door in his face and came back over to us...

"Oh my God – I'm so happy for you guys!" she exclaimed...

"Thank you..." I sighed...

"Why didn't you tell me – never mind - that was a stupid question – le'me get these forms - I'm so damn happy for y'all..."

"Thank you Victoria – that means a lot..." Darnell said...

"Please – don't worry about people talkin' 'bout y'all – you're married – that's all that matters!"

126

"Damn right that's all that matters..." Darnell said as he pulled me into a kiss...

"I'm glad you're so happy for us..." I sighed...

"I am! You had a nice vacation – you got a new job – you got a new husband – Happy New Year!" she exclaimed...

"Happy New Year!" we both exclaimed...

"Okay Darnell – I'll start with you – I know you want your wife on your beneficiary on your pension and life insurance..."

"Absolutely..."

"Okay – is it Chelle Robinson-Tompkins?"

"Chelle Tompkins..." I corrected...

"Okay – you need a new tax form – married and 1 or married and 2?"

"Married and 2..."

"Okay – your social security card stays the same, you ID stays the same – sign these and I'll process them for you...

"I need to change my address..."

"You moved?"

"I moved in with my wife..." he answered as he took my hand...

"Okay – fill this out and I'll get that updated too..." she said as she handed him a change of address form. Darnell filled it out, signed it, and gave it back to her...

"Okay – you're all set – now let's get your paperwork done Mrs. Tompkins..." she said as I started crying...

"No! We left the tissues at home!" Darnell exclaimed...

"I have tissues!" Victoria exclaimed as she handed me some tissues and we bust out laughing...

"What's so funny?"

"Nothing..." we both answered as we bust out laughing again...

"Le'me get this paperwork together..." she laughed as she took out the papers... "Okay Mrs. Tompkins – this one is to change your name..." I took the form from her, filled it out, and gave it back to her...

"Your social security number stays the same so we don't need a copy of that – but make sure you change your name with social security..."

"Okay..."

"Your address is the same so you don't need that – but you'll need to fill out a new tax form..."

"Married and zero..." I said as I took the tax form, filled it out, and gave it back to her...

"Okay – I'll process these for payroll – here's the form for you to change your beneficiary..." she said as she put the form in front of me. I sat there and started crying again...

"What's wrong?" Darnell asked...

"I've never had a beneficiary before..."

"Aww..." Victoria sighed as I filled out the paperwork...

"And this one is for your insurance..." she said as she handed the form to me. I filled it out and gave it back to her...

"Okay – that's all I need for now – I'm treating you both to Kanopi for dinner – Don't bother refusing either because I won't hear it!" she exclaimed as she took out a certificate for Kanopi, filled in a dollar amount, and handed it to Darnell...

"Victoria..."

"Ah Ah Ah! What'd I say?"

"Yes Maam..." he laughed as he showed me the certificate. My eyes got really wide when I saw that the dollar amount she filled in was $500...

"Thank you..." I sniffed...

"You're welcome – are you going back to work?"

"Yes we are..." Darnell answered...

"Okay – Have a great day – if you need anything at all – let me know..."

"We will..." Darnell said as we got up and left her office... "C'mon – let's take the back elevator..." he suggested...

"Okay..." I sighed. When we got in the elevator he pulled me close to him and held me...

"We did it Mrs. Tompkins..."

"Yes we did Mr. Tompkins..." We got off the elevator on the 2nd floor so we could leave out the back door. Darnell took my hand, walked me to Quarropas Street, and then down Court Street to my building...

"Have a good day Mrs. Tompkins..." he breathed as he kissed me...

"Have a good day Mr. Tompkins..." I breathed as I kissed him back...

"I'll see you tonight..." he breathed as he kissed me again...

"See you tonight..." I breathed as I kissed him again. Darnell let go of my hand and walked down Court Street. I turned to go in the building and saw that Ron had been watching us. I walked past him without speaking, went into the building, and got on the elevator. When I got upstairs, Ron was getting off the 2nd elevator at the same time. I opened the door, held the door open for him, and went inside...

"Hey Chelle..."

"Hey Veronica..."

"We doin' lunch today?"

"Yea..."

"Okay – I can't go until 1 today – is that alright?"

"Le'me go check with Steph..."

"Okay – let me know..." she said as she put her head down and continued with her work...

"Good morning Steph..." I greeted...

"Good morning..."

"Is it okay if I go to lunch at 1 this afternoon?"

"Make it 1:30 – Ron's going at 12:30..."

"I'll ask him if he can go at 12..." I said as I left Steph's office and went to Ron's desk...

"Good morning Ron – could you do me a favor and go to lunch today at 12 instead of 12:30?"

"Why do I have to change my lunch hour – I've been going at 12:30 ever since I've been here – now all of a sudden because you're my supervisor I gotta change my lunch hour – this is some bullshit!" he exclaimed as he slammed his hand on his desk. Before I could say anything Steph was behind me...

"Ron – that's enough!"

"See – that's the bullshit I'm talking about right there – you know I always go to lunch at 12:30! Why don't you tell her that?!"

"Ron – I'm warning you..." Steph advised...

"You gonna write me up?! Because I refuse to change my lunch hour?! I'm leaving for the day – then I can go to lunch now if I want to – she thinks she can come in here and do whatever she wants because she's fuckin' Dana's husband – yea – I said it!!" Steph stormed into his office and slammed the door...

"First of all – I asked you if you could do me a favor – I never told you that you had to change your lunch hour – second – I'm not fuckin' anybody's' husband – and if I were – it wouldn't be any of your fuckin' business!"

"Oh yea?! Since you're not fuckin' Dana's husband – why do I have this picture?!" he exclaimed as he shoved his phone in my face. As much as I wanted to cringe, I couldn't – so instead I bust out laughing...

"Nice picture – could you send me a copy of that? My husband would love to see it..."

"Your husband?! Since when?!"

"That's none of your fuckin' business!!" I laughed as I walked away from him and went into Steph's office...

"Are you okay?"

"I'm fine..." I laughed...

"So... I guess congratulations are in order?"

"Yea..."

"Wow... okay... so... about Ron..."

"I'm writing him up..."

"Let me do it..."

"Let me do it – I'll run it by you – if you approve it I'll cc you..."

"Okay..." he answered as I started to leave...

"Oh – I almost forgot – if he leaves for the day – can I still go to lunch with Veronica at 1?"

"Sure – but I need the monthly report before you go..."

"I'll get on that right after I write Ron up..." I said as I went to my desk...

"Girl!" Veronica exclaimed...

"Hold on – I'm getting ready to write Ron up..."

"Oh shit!"

"Steph said I can go to lunch with you at 1..."

"Okay – does he really have a picture of you with Darnell?"

"Yea..."

"How'd he get it?"

"Hell if I know..." I answered as I turned on my computer...

"Yes Stephen?" Victoria answered...

"We have a problem..."

"Oh no! Chelle's not working out?"

"Chelle's fine ‑ Ron's the one that's giving her a hard time..."

"Is she filing a complaint?"

"No – but she is writing him up..."

"Are you backing her up?"

"Absolutely..."

"Good – that'll make my job easier..."

"I need to give you a heads up on something..."

"What?"

"Ron told Chelle she thinks she can do whatever she wants because she's fuckin' Dana's husband..."

"WHAT?! He just blurted that out?!"

"Yes – and from what I heard – he has a picture of them together..."

"He should be fired!!"

"Chelle told him she's not fuckin' anybody's husband and when Ron showed her the picture, she told him Darnell is her husband..."

"He is – they just got married..."

"So that's why she wasn't upset..."

"I need to see this picture..."

"She doesn't know I heard him..."

"Shit!!"

"I'll ask her about it when she brings me the write-up..."

"Okay – get back to me ASAP..."

"Let me see... Ronald Nelson..." I sighed as I searched Facebook... "I found you..." I said as I clicked on his page... "Oohhh... what do we have here?" I asked as I scrolled through his statuses...

"She acting like her shit don't stink – what is she doing with him?" I smiled as I looked at the photo and the comments underneath...

"Oh my God! What?!"

"Isn't that Dana's husband?!"

"Oohhh... Dana's gonna beat that ass!"

"This was posted January 5th..." I whispered...

"This Bitch needs to go back to wherever the hell she came from!"

"Who?" somebody commented...

135

"My new supervisor..."

"This Bitch is really getting on my nerves –
I can't stand her!"

I hit Control/Alt/Delete and printed the
screen as quickly as I could. I right-clicked on
the picture, saved it to the computer, attached it
to an email, sent it to myself, and then I began to
draft a memo...

To: Ronald Nelson
From: Chelle Tompkins
Date: Monday, January 23rd, 2023
Subject: Insubordination, Defamation, Stalking

As per our conversation on Thursday,
January 5th, you have continued to be belligerent
when you are spoken to. Not only has your
attitude affected your work, it has also affected
the moral of other employees in the unit.

Earlier today, I asked you if you could do
me a favor and go to lunch at 12 and you went
ballistic. Not only were you yelling, you were also
using profanity and when Stephen warned you,
you responded by stating that I think I can do
whatever I want because I'm f..... someone else's
husband. After I clarified that I asked you to do
me a favor and I also told you that whoever I was
f...... was none of your business, you jumped up

from your desk and showed me a picture of me and my husband – a picture that was taken on December 24th at the Westchester County Airport.

The attached page from Facebook removes any doubt that you have a personal vendetta against me and the comments that were made after you posted the picture of me with my husband is proof that you've been stalking me.

I am filing a formal complaint against you for harassing me and stalking me, and I am also recommending that you be terminated effective immediately.

Cc: Stephen Richardson
       County Personnel
       Conrad Cox, Attorney

I printed out the memo, picked up what I printed from Ron's page in Facebook, and went into Steph's office...

"Did you finish the monthly report?"
"I haven't started it yet..." I sighed as I handed him the memo I drafted along with what I printed off Facebook. Steph didn't say anything. He took out a pen, signed the memo, and gave it back to me along with the attachment...
"Thank you..."

"You're welcome – can I get the monthly report now?"

"Sure..." I answered as I went over to the copy machine, signed the memo, made the appropriate copies, and made sure I put the original memo on Ron's desk...

"Yes Stephen?" Victoria answered...
"It's worse than we thought..."
"Is the filing a formal complaint?"
"Absolutely..."
"I guess I'll be seeing him in a few minutes..."
"Yes you will..." Steph answered as Ron jumped up from his desk and stormed out the office...

"Hey..." I answered...
"What's wrong?" Darnell asked...
"I'm filing a formal complaint against an employee..."
"What happened?! Are you alright?!"
"I'm okay..."
"No you're not – I'm on my way..."
"Darnell – Don't come up here..."
"Why not?!"
"I'm going to lunch with Veronica..."
"Oh you wanna tell her we got married anyway..." he laughed...
"She already knows..."
"What?! Damn – that didn't take long..."

"Can I call you back?"

"You don't wanna talk to me?"

"I need to finish the monthly report before I go to lunch..."

"I love you..."

"I love you more..." I said as I hung up and went back to working on the monthly report...

"Welcome to Haiku – Oh you here to see your friend..." she laughed as I went over to the table...

"How'd you get here before me?" I asked as I sat down...

"I left a few minutes early..."

"No you didn't..."

"I just told you..."

"You took your break at 12:45 because you didn't get a chance to take a break this morning..." I interrupted...

"Yes Maam!" she laughed...

"You know I wrote Ron up – right?"

"Can I see it?"

"I can't show you what I wrote – but I bet you if you listen to Ron later you'll know exactly what I said...

"You don't trust me?"

"I trust you – but when I tell personnel that I haven't shared the complaint with anyone else – I need that to be the truth..."

"Here you go..." the waiter said as he put the shumi on the table with our vodka shots...

"You know I'm still mad at you – right?"

"Yes..."

"So how's married life?"

"I'm so damn happy..." I sighed...

"Well I'm glad you're happy – I still don't think you should've married him but anyway – are you moving?"

"Nope..."

"He's moving here?"

"Yup..."

"Please tell me he's getting his own place..."

"He moved in with me..."

"Did you sign a pre-nup?"

"Can we toast?"

"What are we toasting too?"

"Thank God we're married – otherwise my shit would've been blown..."

"Thank God you're married otherwise your shit – nope – not drinking to that..."

"Okay – Here's to Ron being dumb enough to have his settings set to public on Facebook..."

"Oh shit! You saw his page? Did he post the picture?" I didn't answer her question. I smiled and took a shot...

"I'll drink to that!" she exclaimed as she took a shot...

"Here's your food..." the waiter asked as he put our lunch on the table...

"We don't have a pre-nup..."

"Are you crazy?!"

"Nope..."

"He's living in your condo with you?"

"Yup..."

"Thank God that's in your name..."

"Yup..."

"Are you getting a place together?'

"Yup..."

"Make sure your name's on that shit – especially since your mortgage won't be paid off..."

"It'll be paid off..." I said as I smiled...

"It will?!"

"Yea..."

"Okay... I'm not as mad as I was..."

"Good..."

"Nothing against him – I just think you should've waited..."

"I'm glad we didn't..."

"Why?"

"If Ron thinks I was fucking Dana's husband, so do other people..."

"What if people think you were having an affair before his wife died?"

"Especially because that picture was taken on Christmas eve... ooppsss..."

"Wait a minute – Ron was off on Friday..."

"Which Friday?"

"He was off on Friday the 23rd!"

"He didn't know I was transferred to 85 – did he?"

"I'on know – but so what – what was he doing at the airport at 5 a.m. anyway?"

"Maybe he was going to Atlanta for the weekend..."

"I'ma see if I find him on Facebook..." she said as she searched for him... "Oh shit!"

"What?" Veronica didn't say anything – she just showed me her phone so I could read his latest status...

"Fuckin' Bitch filed a complaint against me for defamation and stalking – she's the hoe that was fucking Dana's husband – but I'm on administrative leave without pay for two weeks because I posted a picture on my mutha fucking page - Since you like reading shit I hope you read this – BITCH!"

"Wow..." I sighed as I shook my head and continued eating...

"Somebody needs to tell him he's not helping himself..."

"You know what – you just gave me an idea..."

"What're you gonna do?"

"I'm gonna change the subject..."

"See – that ain't right..."

"You know – I realized that if you're at the copy machine you can hear Steph's conversations – especially when he leaves his door open..."

"Hmmm..."

"Darnell called me earlier..."

"Did you tell him what happened?"

"No – I just said I had to file a complaint against one of my employees...

"Oh shit – what'd he say?"

"I told him I needed to finish the monthly report..."

"You didn't tell him?"

"He was ready to come up here..."

"You should've told him..."

'I'll tell him when I get home..."

"I hope they move Ron's ass!"

"They are..."

"They are?!"

"Steph is backing me up..."

"Yeesss!"

"Oh hey Darnell – I heard you got married – congratulations..." Raymond said as Darnell walked into personnel...

"Thank you..." he replied as he went to Victoria's office...

"Hello Darnell – did you forget something?" Victoria asked...

"My wife told me she had to file a complaint against one of her employees..."

"Darnell..."

"I know you can't discuss it with me..."

"Then why are you here?"

"I was hoping you would anyway..."

"I'm sorry Darnell – I can't – but since you're here – would you like to add your wife to your medical insurance?"

"Doesn't she already have insurance?"

"Yes..."

"So can it stay the way it is?"

"I guess it can – you both work for the County so it shouldn't be a problem..."

"Oh excuse me – I'll wait..." Ron said as he interrupted...

"Hello Ronald – I'm Darnell Tompkins – it's been brought to my attention that you have a problem with my wife..."

"I don't have a problem with your wife – she..."

"Stop it right there!" Victoria snapped... "Darnell – congratulations it was nice to see you – Mr. Nelson – come inside – have a seat..." Darnell got up and left but he didn't go far...

"Ms. Johnson – this isn't right!"

"Mr. Nelson – you made this bed – you have to lay in it – I'm sorry..."

"She's had it in for me from the day she got there – you sent her there on purpose to get me to transfer to Yonkers!"

"Well – since you brought that up – that's where you'll be going..."

"I knew it!"

"Mr. Nelson – you need to take responsibility for your actions – you're lucky you haven't been brought up on a section 75..."

"You know what – I'm done – I'm getting an attorney – thanks for nothing!" he exclaimed as he got up...

"Remember – you're to report to the Yonkers D.O. when you come back from your administrative leave..." she said as Ron stormed out...

"You can come in Darnell..."

"I'm good..."

"Okay – hopefully we can put this to bed – now I need to get on this paperwork to get Mr. Nelson's transfer processed – at least somebody's happy..." she sighed as she started on the paperwork...

"Hello Darnell..." Conrad greeted as he answered his phone...

"Hey Conrad..."

"How's everything?"

"I just got married..."

"What?! When did this happen?!"

"Last week on Tuesday..."

"January 17th?"

"Yes..."

"Wow – Congratulations!!"

"Thank you – I need your help with something..."

"Already?"

"Unfortunately – yes..."

"What happened?"

"My wife is being harassed and stalked by one of her employees..."

"Oh damn! I'm sorry to hear that!"

"She had to file a formal complaint against him for harassment, defamation, and stalking..."

"Damn shame – you should be on your honeymoon..."

"We had our honeymoon before we got married..."

"Really?!"

"Yes – we met in an Uber on our way to the airport..."

"Oh wow!"

"We were both on the same flight to Bermuda – one thing led to another – and now we're married..."

"I'm really happy for you – tell me what I can do to help you..."

"I need this guy to be served today..."

"Served?"

"Yes – he needs a cease & desist order..."

"Do you have documentation to support this?"

"His name is Ronald Nelson – he's been posting a few statuses regarding my wife – and he also posted a picture of us kissing at the airport..."

"What?!"

"That's not all..."

"What else is there?!"

"He's spreading a rumor that my wife is fucking Dana's husband..."

"Do you have his picture?"

"I just text it to you..."

"Where does he work?"

"He works at 85 Court Street in White Plains..."

"I'll get on this right now – he'll be served before 5..."

"Thank you Conrad..."

"You're welcome..."

"Ron – I'm glad you're back – I need to see you in my office..." Steph said...

"I already know – I'm just here to clean out my desk..." he sighed as he began putting items in a box...

"What happened?"

"Please don't insult me – you already know what happened..."

"RONALD NELSON!" Ron dropped the box as Veronica and I turned around in shock. That was the first time we'd ever heard Steph take that tone or call someone's full name...

"Yes?!" Ron answered with his hands on his hips...

"I asked you a question..." Ron rolled his eyes, picked up his box, and continued packing.

Steph stormed into his office and slammed the door shut...

"You got what you wanted – I hope you're happy!" he exclaimed as he picked up his box and started to leave...

"Mr. Nelson?" Officer Sullivan asked as he came in...

"Oh my God! You don't need to arrest me – I'm leaving!"

"Are you Mr. Nelson?"

"Yes – I'm Mr. Nelson!"

"You've been served..." Officer Sullivan said as Steph came out his office...

"What's going on?"

"Who are you?"

"I'm his manager, Stephen Richardson – is he under arrest?"

"No – I'm just here to serve him..." he answered as Ron opened the envelope...

"Oh my God! You gotta be fuckin' kidding me – you know what – you're an EVIL BITCH!!" he exclaimed as he came towards me...

"Get him outta here!" Steph exclaimed...

"Yes Sir!" Officer Sullivan exclaimed as he grabbed Ron by his shoulders...

"Take your fuckin' hands off me!" Ron glared as he turned around...

"Look – you can leave on your own – or you can leave in handcuffs – your choice!"

"I'm leaving!" Ron exclaimed as he picked up his box, threw the letter in it, and stormed out the door with Officer Sullivan right behind him...

"Chelle?"

"Yes Steph?"

"Do you know what that was all about?"

"Actually – No..."

"I'm going over to 112..." he said as he left...

"What the fuck!" Veronica exclaimed...

"I know!"

"You didn't have him served?"

"If I had him served – I'd say that..."

"I'm not accusing you – I'm just asking..."

"I know – but I wish I knew..." I laughed...

"Steph is pissed! I've never seen him like that!"

"I hope he's not pissed at me..."

"I thought you said he backed you up?"

"He did..."

"Hello Stephen – I was just getting ready to call you..."

"Ronald was about to be arrested..."

"WHAT?!"

"He came back to the office and started cleaning out his desk..."

'He's going to Yonkers – I was going to tell you but Darnell came in to see me while Mr. Nelson was here so I didn't get a chance..."

"That explains it..."

"Why was he about to be arrested?"

"Office Sullivan served him papers..."

"How is that even possible? Unless..."

"Unless what?"

"Well... Chelle did cc her attorney on the complaint..."

"That's right..."

"I hope she didn't have Mr. Nelson served while she was in the office..."

"That's why Ronald was about to be arrested – he called her an evil bitch and went at her..."

"Oh my God! Is she alright?!"

"She's fine – but I need to speak to her – if she did that without letting me know that isn't cool..." Victoria sat there thinking for a few moments...

"Chelle didn't have him served – Darnell did..."

"You think so?"

"He came to see me while Mr. Nelson was here. I told him to go wait outside. He hung around until after Mr. Nelson left and when I told him he could come in, he changed his mind and followed Mr. Nelson out..."

"I don't blame him..."

"I don't either – but I hope this mess goes away now that he's been served..."

"Speaking of mess – I need a clerk..."

"I gotcha – I'ma give you Daniel..."

"Who's Daniel?"

"The clerk in Yonkers..."

"Jewish guy, wears glasses?"

"That's him..."

"He's nice – I'll have to let Chelle know she'll need to sit on him a little – once he gets to talking he stops working – but I'll take him over Ronald any day..."

"I'll call Daniel and let him know he'll be starting Monday..."

"Yonkers will be without a clerk for two weeks..."

"They'll have to work it out with who they have – they have too many clerks as it is..."

"I'll see you later – thank you Victoria..." Steph laughed as he got up...

"You're welcome..."

"Chelle – I need to see you in my office..."

"Okay..." I sighed as I got up and went into his office...

"Close the door..." I closed the door and sat down... "I need to ask you something..."

"Okay..."

"Did you know Ron was going to be served today?"

"No – I..."

"Don't say anything else..." he interrupted...

"Okay..."

"You're getting a new clerk on Monday..."

153

"Already?"

"His name is Daniel Malev..."

"We're getting Dan?!"

"You know Daniel?"

"Yea..."

"So you're happy..."

"Oh yea – he used to go to lunch with us when he was at 112 – he's nice..."

"That can't happen here..."

"Really?"

"Okay – maybe he can go to lunch with you and Veronica once in a while – but you can't do more than an hour – we need coverage in the office..."

"Thank you..." I said as I smiled...

"That's it –you can go tell Veronica – oh – before you go – you didn't show Veronica the complaint did you?"

"Steph!"

"I had to ask..."

"Bye..." I said as I got up to leave... "Veronica! Guess what?!" I exclaimed as I hurried out his office. Steph just shook his head and laughed to himself...

"Hey..." I sighed when I saw Darnell. Darnell pulled me into his arms and kissed me hard... "Darnell... Stop..."

"Why?"

"You can't kiss me like that in public – not here anyway..."

"I'll kiss my wife anywhere I want..." he breathed as he kissed my neck... "However I want..." he breathed as he kissed me again...

"Get a room!" Someone exclaimed as all the clients laughed...

"C'mon..." I laughed as I took his hand and pulled him down Court Street...

"Good evening Ms. Robinson..." Robert greeted...

"Mrs. Tompkins..." Darnell corrected as he moved me towards the elevator...

"You're in a hurry..." I laughed. Darnell didn't respond. I shrugged my shoulders and waited for the elevator to get to our floor. Darnell took my hand, pulled me out of the elevator and sped-walked to our door...

"You're really in a hurry!" I laughed again. Darnell opened the door, pulled me inside, and pushed the door closed...

"Go sit down..." I didn't like his tone one bit but I also knew I had better do what he told me... "Don't ever do that to me again..."

"What did I do?"

"When I called you today – I asked you what was wrong and instead of telling me what was going on –you rushed me off the phone..."

"I needed to finish the monthly report..."

"And that was more important than me?!"

"No – I would've had the monthly report finished earlier but I had to write Ron up..."

"Why didn't you tell me what happened?!"

"I was going to tell you tonight when we got home..." I sighed...

"I'm sorry – I thought you were trying to keep it from me..."

"I wanted to handle it myself before I told you – I don't want people thinking that I need to run to my husband whenever something happens..."

"I thought you didn't give a damn what anyone said about you and me?"

"I don't – but when he showed me that picture – I couldn't let him know he got to me – nobody would respect me if I let that happened..." I said as I started crying...

"I'm sorry..." he sighed as he pulled me into a hug...

"Steph wanted to write him up but I told him to let me do it – I needed to show him that I could handle myself – especially as a supervisor..."

"I'm sorry – I didn't think about that – I just reacted..."

"You had Ron served - didn't you?"

"Yes..."

"Steph and I had no idea what was going on..."

"So he was served?"

"Ron started cleaning out his desk. I just figured he was put on administrative leave so I didn't question him but when Steph asked him what happened he got mad..."

"He got mad?"

"Yes – he thought Steph knew he was being transferred..."

"That must be why he went to see Victoria..."

"How do you know about that?"

"I know about that because I went to see Victoria..."

"Oh no! She told you?"

"Relax Chelle – she told me she couldn't discuss your complaint with me – but I introduced myself to Ron – and I told him it's been brought to my attention that you have a problem with my wife..."

"Oh Darnell..." I sighed...

"I'm sorry – but I'll step to anybody that comes for you – even it if costs me my job!"

"I love you..."

"You're not mad?"

"Hell no – but you're about to be..."

"What happened?!"

"Promise me you won't do anything..."

"I can't promise you that..."

"Well... Officer Sullivan served Ron the papers..."

"You were there?"

"Yes... and..."

"What happened?!"

"Ron read the papers and... he called me an evil bitch..." Darnell was sitting there seething. His eyes turned to slits, he started breathing heavy, and his nostrils flared... "Darnell... please calm down..." I said as I touched his hand...

"Is he coming back to work?"

"No – as soon as he came towards me Steph told Officer Sullivan to get him out of there..."

"So... What you're telling me is... He came towards you?"

"Yes..."

"After he called you an evil bitch?!"

"Yes..."

"Thank you for telling me..." he said as he stood up...

"Where are you going?"

"I'll be right back..." he answered as he went into the office and closed the door...

"Hello Darnell..."

"I have a problem..."

"What's wrong? He didn't get served?"

"He threatened my wife..."

"When?!"

"After he got served, he called my wife an evil bitch and then he stepped to her..."

"Where there any witnesses?"

"Her manager was there and so was Officer Sullivan..."

"That's good – if this goes to court he's handing your wife a settlement..."

"He better pray he makes it to court..."

"Darnell – listen to me..."

"I'm listening..."

"I need you to stay away from him..."

"I know..."

"I'm serious – I need you to stay away from him..."

"That's not going to be easy..."

"Why not?"

"He was transferred to my office..."

"Are you okay?" I asked as Darnell came out of the office...

"I'm sorry – I needed a minute to calm down...

"Are you upset with me?"

"I'm not upset with you – I love you..."

"You scared me..."

"I didn't mean to – I'm sorry..."

"Who were you talking too?"

"I was talking to Conrad..."

"Ohh..."

"I told him Ron got transferred to my office..."

"Ron got transferred to Yonkers?!"

"Yea..."

"Did you ask Victoria to do that?"

"No..."

"Is he going to be reporting to you?"

"No..."

"Good..."

"But I'm going to make sure he knows who I am..."

"Darnell..."

"I'm done talking about him..." he breathed as he pulled me into a kiss...

"Mmm... Okay..."

"Let's go to Kanopi for dinner..." he suggested as he took my hand and walked me towards the door...

"Okay..." I sighed...

"Welcome to Kanopi – Can I start you off with something to drink?"

"Yes – I'll have the zorro's daiquiri..."

"Are you Mr. & Mrs. Tompkins?"

"Yes we are – why?"

"Robert told us how much you enjoyed our drink – and he told us you got married – Congratulations..."

"Thank you..."

"What can I get for you Mrs. Tompkins?"

"I'll have the pomegranate spritzer..."

"I'll be right back..." he said as he went to get our drinks...

"I had no idea this place was so nice..." Darnell sighed...

"I've never been to one of their lofts..."

"Really?"

161

"No – I never had a reason to go before now..." I answered as the waiter brought our drinks to the table...

"Would you like to hear what we have on the chef's tasting menu?"

"Yes please..." we both answered...

"Okay – Tonight's menu consists of the following...

"Grilled Cheese & Crab, sapateira, lime mayo..."

"That sounds good..." I said...

"Himachi yellowtail amberjack, citrus avocado, aged soy piri piri..."

"That's sounds good..." Darnell said...

"Mozambique Tiger Shrimp, parsley, garlic, and crushed red pepper..."

"That sounds really good!" I exclaimed...

"Seaweed Linguini, scarlet prawns..."

"I need to see that!" Darnell exclaimed...

"Bacalhau A Pil Pil, black olive-squid ink, chocos..."

"Squid?!" we both exclaimed...

"Steak Pica Pau, rib eye, vinegar..."

"That's more like it..." Darnell said...

"Iberian Port Presa, yukon gold potato, xo sauce...

"Okay..." I said...

"Marcona Almond Ice Cream, warm chocolate sauce, toasted almond ice..."

"That sounds good..." Darnell sighed as he picked up his spoon, licked it, and winked at me...

"I'll be right back..." the waiter said as we finished our drinks...

"This should be interesting..." I said. We sat there and waited for the waiter to bring out our first course..."

"Well – at least we don't have to worry about getting full..." I said as he put the grilled cheese & crab on the table...

"Hmmm – this is actually pretty good..." Darnell said as he tasted it...

"You're right..." I agreed. We laughed each time the waiter walked away at the size of the plates and servings...

"How was everything?" the waiter asked...

"Interesting..." we both answered...

"I'll be back with the check..." he said as he walked away. We couldn't hold it in any longer...

"Ahh Haa Haa Haa Haa Haa! Ahh Haa Haa Haa Haa Haa!"

"Here's your check..."

"Here's your certificate..." Darnell said as he put the certificate down on the table before the waiter could walk away..."

"I'll take care of this and bring you the difference..." the waiter said as he walked away. We got up from the table and went to look out the window...

"I like the view from our bedroom much better..." Darnell sighed...

"So do I..."

"Mr. Tompkins?" the waiter startled us...

"Yes?" Darnell answered as we turned around...

"Here's your credit – have a good evening..." he said as he handed Darnell another certificate...

"Hmmm... $200..."

"Oh boy..." I sighed as I rubbed my stomach..."

"What's wrong?"

"I don't feel so good..." I answered as I hurried out the restaurant and he followed behind me. When we got upstairs I rushed to our door, opened it, and rushed into the 1st bathroom... "Uuuggghhh!"

"Are you alright?"

"Maybe the sushi wasn't such a good idea..."

"Umm... I think you're right!" he exclaimed as he hurried to the office bathroom... "Uuuggghhh!" Unfortunately the rest of the evening   didn't   get   any   better.

"Good morning..." Darnell breathed as he kissed me awake...

"Good morning..."

"How are you feeling?"

"I'm feeling better than I was last night..."

"I hope Victoria doesn't ask how Kanopi was..."

"If she asks, we'll tell her we had a great time, the drinks were good, we loved the views, and the food was good..."

"That's not true..."

"The food was good – we just couldn't handle sushi, steak cooked medium rare, and pork cooked medium..."

"Exactly..." he agreed as he got up...

"Where are you going?" I asked...

"I'm going to the bathroom..."

"Why are you going to the office?"

"You don't want me to blow up this one – trust me..." he laughed as he went towards the office. Good thing he didn't want to blow up the master bathroom because just as he was leaving, my stomach started bubbling...

"You want me to make coffee?"

"No – I'll get some outside..."

"Are you sure?"

"Yea..."

"Okay – c'mon – I'll walk you out and then I'll head to Yonkers..." he said as he held the door open for me...

"Good morning Mr. & Mrs. Tompkins..." Robert greeted...

"Good morning..." we both said...

"Have a good day..." Darnell said...

"Thank you – same to you..." Robert replied...

"Have a good day Mr. Tompkins..." I sighed as I pulled him into a kiss...

"Have a good day Mrs. Tompkins..." he breathed as he kissed me back. Darnell watched me walk away before he went to go get the car...

"Good morning!" I exclaimed as I walked in...

"Chelle!" Dan exclaimed...

"Hey Chelle..." Veronica greeted...

"You work 8:30 to 4:30?" Dan asked...

"No – I just like to come in early so I have time to enjoy my breakfast and coffee..."

"What time does everybody go to lunch?"

"I'll talk to you at 9..." I answered as I went out the door and went into the break room...

"You alright?" Veronica asked as she came in...

"Yea..."

"You sure?"

"We had dinner at Kanopi..."

"I heard they have good food..."

"They have good food – but our stomachs couldn't handle sushi, steak cooked medium rare, or pork cooked medium..."

"Why'd you eat it then?!"

"We didn't know we couldn't handle it until after we tried it..."

"Oh – feel better..."

"Thanks – I hope I can keep this coffee down..."

"You should've got a cup of tea..." she said as she left...

"Good morning...." Steph greeted as he walked in...

"Good morning Mr. Richardson..." Dan greeted...

"You can call me Steph..."

"Good morning Steph..."

"Is Chelle in yet?"

"She's in the break room..." Veronica answered...

"Okay Dan – let's talk..." I said as I walked back in...

"Steph's looking for you..." Veronica said...

"Okay..."

"Good morning Chelle..." Steph greeted...

"Good morning..."

"They're short downstairs and they'd like Veronica to cover reception..."

"I'll send Dan..."

"They asked for Veronica..."

"If we start that – they'll never stop..."

"Okay – send Dan – but if they start complaining we'll have to put Veronica back in the rotation..."

"I hope not..." I sighed as I left his office...

"Dan – we'll have to talk later – they need coverage in reception..."

"Okay..." he said as he got up... "I'll see you later..." Veronica waited for him to leave before she spoke..."

"You know they don't like him down there – right?"

"I know – they don't like how friendly he is – they want him to hurry people along – but that's not Dan's personality..."

"I hope they don't start complaining..."

"I hope they don't either because if they start complaining Steph said I have to put you back in the rotation." Veronica rolled her eyes and went back to doing her work...

"Good morning..." Darnell greeted...

"Hey! I heard you got married – Congratulations!" Frances exclaimed...

"Thank you..."

"Ron's here..."

"He is?"

"Yes..."

"He's on administrative leave for two weeks – he's not supposed to be here..."

"Oh shoot – he's unpacking now – I'll go stop him..."

"That's alright – let him un-pack – I'll go say hello..." Darnell said as he went towards Frances' office and she followed...

"Good morning..." he greeted when he saw Ron. Ron looked at him and his eyes got as big as if he was a deer caught in headlights... "Welcome to Yonkers..."

"Thanks..." Ron mumbled...

Frances – make sure you add Ron to the rotation for reception..."

"Yes sir..."

"I'm not due to start for two weeks! Can't I get settled first? Damn!"

"Who the fuck you think you talkin' too?!" Frances exclaimed...

"I'm just saying..."

"Let me tell you one muthafuckin' thing right now Ron – I'm not the one!"

"Are you gonna let her talk to me like that?" Ron asked as he looked at Darnell...

"Isn't that how you spoke to my wife?" Frances looked at Darnell in shock...

"I'm done – I'll be back in two weeks..." Ron sighed as he got up and left...

"This is going to work out just fine..." Darnell laughed...

"I hope you didn't set me up Darnell..."

"I had nothing to do with this – he did this to himself – and he got you – and you'll make sure he works..."

"Oh hell yea – we all work down here – ain't no slackin!" she laughed...

"I'll see you later..." Darnell laughed as he went back to his office...

"Who the hell is this?!" Ron exclaimed as he looked at his phone... "Hello?"

"Is this Mr. Nelson?"

"Yes – who is this?"

"This is Mr. Cox from the Cox Law Firm..."

"I'm not speaking to you!" Ron exclaimed as he disconnected the call. The phone rang again... "Hello?!"

"Mr. Nelson – Please don't hang up on me again..."

"I don't have to speak to you..."

"You're right – but I think you should speak to me – you can't afford not to..."

"What's that supposed to mean?"

"We need to meet in person..."

"Why?"

"Mr. Nelson – I'm not your enemy..."

"You represent Chelle Robinson!"

"I represent Chelle Tompkins..."

"Whatever..."

"Can we meet?"

"Why – so you can have me arrested?"

"Mr. Nelson – I'm not trying to have you arrested – I'm trying to help you..."

"Why would you be trying to help me?"

"If you'll agree to meet with me, we can discuss it..."

"Where are you located?"

"Are you able to come to Yonkers?"

"I'm in Yonkers now..."

"I'm at 30 Larkin Plaza..."

"I'm on my way..."

"Thank you for coming in..."

"Okay – I'm here – What do you wanna talk about?"

"Well... I'm afraid I don't have good news..."

"I knew it – I shouldn't've come here..."

"Mr. Nelson – Please – Listen..."

"Alright – I'm listening..."

"Mrs. Tompkins has a good case..."

"How? I never harassed her, stalked her, or threatened her!"

"According to the legal definition – that's exactly what you did..."

"According to the legal definition?!"

"Let me explain..."

"Go 'head!" Ron exclaimed as he threw up his hands...

"There are two types of harassment: harassment and aggravated harassment. Aggravated harassment is physical assault and damage to property in the first and second degree..."

"I never did any of that..."

"I agree; however, you are guilty of harassment in the first degree..."

"First degree?"

"Yes – harassment in the second degree is where you do it repeatedly or you strike them..."

"You know I didn't do that – right?"

"We're here to discuss what you actually did..."

"So what – I can't get mad or voice my opinion without worrying about someone suing me?!"

"Mr. Nelson – you were belligerent after you were warned..."

"I was pissed! Haven't you ever been pissed?!"

"Of course – but this was with your supervisor – and there were witnesses..."

"This isn't right!"

"According to New York Penal Law 240.25 – it's right... and that's not all..."

"What else is there?"

"You posted in social media..."

"I can post whatever I want on my page!"

"Yes – you can post whatever you want on your page – but I'm sure you realize by now that there are consequences to doing that..."

"I wasn't even stalking them! I was on my way to Atlanta for the weekend and I saw them – I took the picture because I thought I was catching him cheating on his wife!"

"First – let me give you some advice – if this goes to court – and there's a good chance it will – don't repeat what you just told me – second – your comments along with the picture you posted made this situation a lot worse...."

"I wish I never took that picture..." he sighed...

"I wish you never took the picture – I wish you never showed it to her – and I wish you never made that comment..."

"I wish I never did this either – from now on I don't care what I see – I'm minding my business!"

"That's nice to hear – but we still have a problem – this may go to court..."

"What happens if this goes to court?"

"The limit on damages for unlawful workplace harassment claims is $300,000..."

"WHAT?!"

"And she can also sue you for attorney fees, missed days from work, and stress..."

"Stress?!

"You don't think this situation is stressful?"

"Hell yea it's stressful – stressful to me!"

"It amazes me that you can see stress because of what happened to you – but you can't see the stress you caused her..."

"You're her lawyer so you're gonna side with her no matter what I say..."

"Okay – I'm done trying to talk to you – here are your only options – you agree to settle for $50,000 or you take your chances in court..."

"$50,000?! I don't have $50,000!"

"I know you don't have it – but I also know you can get it..."

"Where am I supposed to get that kind of money?!"

"You can take a loan from your pension..."

"Now I know why you wanted me to come see you – you don't give a damn about me – you just wanna get paid!"

"If I only cared about money I'd convince my client to refuse a settlement and take this to court..."

"So if I agree to settle this... Can she still get me fired?"

"Once this is settled – I'm sure I can convince my client to move on from that – especially since she's a newlywed..."

"So they're really married?"

"Yes..."

"So if I agree to settle this – what happens at work?"

"I'll let your employer know my client has reached a settlement and we won't need to communicate with them after that..."

"How much time do I have?"

"I'll wait to hear from you..."

"So you haven't scheduled a court date yet?"

"I shouldn't be telling you this..." Conrad whispered as he leaned towards Ron...

"Tell me what?"

"My client doesn't want this to go to court but..."

"But what?"

"Her husband wants it to go to court..."

"Dammit!"

"Don't worry about him – you get back to me and I'll take care of Mr. Tompkins..."

"Okay – I'll get back to you..." Ron sighed as he got up and left the office...

"Hello Conrad..." Darnell sighed...

"It's done..."

"It's done?"

"He just left..."

"How'd it go?"

"It didn't take much to convince him – once I told him he was guilty according to the New York Penal Law – it was pretty easy after that..."

"I'm glad to hear that..."

"I poured it on a little thicker by confiding in him that she doesn't want to go to court but you do..."

"Oh no! Why'd you tell him that? That was confidential!" Darnell laughed...

"Good afternoon..." I said as I answered my cell...

"Mrs. Tompkins – I have good news for you..."

"You do?"

"Mr. Nelson has agreed to settle so you don't have to go to court..."

"Oh thank God!"

"I'm waiting for him to get back to me so there's no money yet – but I got him to agree to a settlement for $50,000!"

"$50,000?! Wow!"

"As soon as I hear from him I'll notify your employer that my client has agreed to a settlement and then you can go back to enjoying being a newlywed..."

 "I can't wait to tell Darnell!"

 "He already knows..."

 "He does?"

 "Yes..."

 "Thank you Conrad..."

 "You're welcome – have a nice day..."

"Hey!" Darnell exclaimed when he saw me...

"Surprise!" I exclaimed as I ran over to him and jumped in his arms. Darnell kissed me, picked me up, and spun me around...

"What brings you here?"

"Okay... Please don't get mad..."

"Why would I get mad?"

"Because..." I sighed as I sat down... I just came from Conrad's office..."

"You got the check! Le'me see!" I took the envelope out my purse and handed it to him. I watched him open the envelope and look at the amount... "$33,500! Yeeessss! We need to go celebrate..."

"Darnell..."

"What's wrong?"

"Well..."

"You don't want the check..." he sighed as he slumped down in his chair..."

"I knew you'd be mad..."

"I'm not mad... I just don't understand..."

"I know Ron needs to pay for what he did..."

"Yes!"

"I wanted him to pay... and he did..."

"You don't want the check!"

"Darnell... Listen..."

"I'm listening..." he sighed...

"Before we met, something was missing in my life... something big..." Darnell started smiling and I couldn't help it...

"I'm not talking about that!" I laughed...

"I didn't say anything!"

"God brought us together before we made it to the airport..."

"Yes he did..."

"We love each other...

"Yes we do..."

"We thank God for each other..."

"Yes we do..."

"We're married..."

"Yes we are..."

"We're happy..."

"Yes we are..."

"We have a wonderful life ahead of us... In spite of everything that happened..."

"Yes we do... but I have to ask..."

"What does this have to do with Ron..." I sighed...

"Yes..."

"Well... Ron got written up..."

"As he should've..."

"Ron got disciplined..."

"As he should've..."

"Ron got transferred..."

"As he should've..."

"Ron had to pay..."

"As he should've..."

"I think he's paid enough..."

"If you give him back this check, he hasn't paid anything..."

"He paid $16,500..."

"I forgot about that..."

"It's not about the money – it's the principle..."

"What do you mean it's the principle?"

"Ron suffered consequences for his actions. He got written up, disciplined, transferred, and had to pay a settlement. I think the lesson was learned...."

"Okay – I'll give him the benefit of the doubt... a little..."

"So you understand why I want to give him the check?"

"I understand... when you're happy you tend to see the world through rose-colored glasses..."

"I've always seen the world that way... according to my mother..." Darnell got up from his chair, came from behind the desk, and pulled me up into a kiss, and gave me back the envelope...

"If you want to give him the check, give it to him..."

"So... You're okay with it?"

"I love you..." he laughed...

"I love you too – what's so funny?"

"Nothing – go give Ron the check – when you're done come back here and I'll take you to lunch...

"Good morning! Congratulations!" Frances greeted when she saw me...

"Good morning - Thank you – is Ron here?"

"His desk is right on the other side of that cubicle..." she answered...

"Thanks..." I said as I walked around on the other side of the cubicle...

"What are you doing here?!" he exclaimed...

"Good morning – is there somewhere we can talk?"

"I'm done talking to you..."

"Okay – Is there somewhere we can go so I can talk and you can listen?"

"I'm not interested in anything you have to say! Please leave me alone!"

"Ron?" Darnell asked behind me. Ron's eyes got big and I turned around to look at him...

"Yes Mr. Tompkins?" Darnell responded as he stood up and put his hands on his hips...

"Please meet my wife in the conference room..."

"This is harassment – I'll meet your wife in the conference room – but I'm filling a complaint – I shouldn't have to put up with this!" he exclaimed...

"What's going on?" Frances asked as she came over to us...

"My wife came to see Ron..." Darnell answered...

"What's the problem Ron?" Frances asked...

"I just want to be left alone! I don't want to meet with either one of them!"

"Ron – go see what she has to say – she came to Yonkers to see you when she could've called on the phone – it must be important..."

"I don't have to meet with her if I don't want to! I don't give a damn what you or anybody else says!"

"Please?" Frances asked... "For me?"

"Fine – I'll go – for you!" Ron snapped as he stormed off towards the conference room...

"Thank you Ron..." I said as I closed the door...

"Why are you here? You wrote me up, I lost two weeks' pay, you got me transferred, and you got your settlement – haven't I suffered enough?!"

"Yes you have..." I answered as I handed him the envelope...

"What's this – another complaint?!"

"Open it..." Ron opened the envelope and took out the check...

"Unbelievable! You got $33,500 – and instead of depositing it you came down here to rub it in my face?! That's why you wanted to see me?!"

"Ron – look at the back of the check..." I waited for Ron to look at the back of the check...

"Pay to the order of Ronald Nelson..." he read as he teared up...

"Now do you understand?"

"Oh my God... Thank you Jesus..." he cried...

"Thank you Jesus..." I sighed as I opened the door, left him in the conference room, and headed back to Darnell's office...

"Frances – I'm going to lunch..." he said as we left. We went to Julios on Park Hill and even though I gave Ron the check, it didn't stop us from celebrating before I went back to work...

"Hey..." I breathed as soon as I saw Darnell...

"Hey..." he breathed as he pulled me into a kiss...

"Get a room!" somebody yelled...

"Leave 'em alone!" somebody else yelled...

"C'mon..." Darnell said as he took my hand and we started walking down Court Street...

"Bye Ms. Robinson!" somebody yelled...

"Mrs. Tompkins!" Darnell corrected...

"Good evening Mr. & Mrs. Tompkins..." Robert greeted...

"Good evening Robert..." we both greeted...

"Have a good night..."

"You too..." we both said as we went inside and got in the elevator...

"I love you Mrs. Tompkins..." he breathed as he pulled me into a kiss...

"I love you too Mr. Tompkins..." I said as I kissed him back. We got to our floor, got off the elevator, went to our door, opened it, and went inside... "Where are you going?" I asked...

"I'll be right back..." he answered as he went into the office. I made him a drink, poured myself some moscato, and took the drinks into the living room. When he came out of the office, I was sitting on the couch and the drinks were on the table...

"What are you up to?"

"You'll see..." he answered as he put the tablet on the table next to the flat screen and connected it...

"Oh Darnell..." I sighed as the video from our wedding day started playing. Darnell added the pictures before the wedding to the beginning

185

of our video followed by more pictures after our video. I began to cry when I realized he also added the video of us on the yacht. Darnell sat down beside me, picked up his drink, and wrapped his arm around me as we watched ourselves... "You looked so damn good..." I sighed...

"So did you..."

"I had no idea you could sing..."

"I had no idea you could sing..."

"Look at us..." I sighed as I pointed to the flat screen...

"You loved every bit of it..." he said as we watched him fucking me behind the counter...

"I can't believe we did that..."

"We brought in the New Year just the way I wanted..." he breathed as he kissed me...

"We sure did..." I breathed as he put down his glass and pushed me down on the couch....

<u>Discussion</u>

Do you agree with Chelle's decision to give Ron the check? Why or why not?